Her Bi
Inconveni

MW00438571

He needs a temporary wife to save his business and his parent's legacy, she needs money to save her dream...will an inconvenient wedding be a blessing of love?

Beck McCoy would have given up every cent of his inheritance to have his mother and father back from the fatal plane crash that killed them when he was a boy. Instead of being afraid to fly he grew up obsessed with flying. It has always been his connection to his father, who also loved to be in the sky. Part owner of a private jet charter service he loves every moment of it. When his grandfather demands he find a bride or lose his inheritance, the legacy his dad and mom helped build for him, Beck is furious but determined to do whatever it takes. He must marry or start from scratch-- something he's not afraid to do but losing the inheritance from his parents makes his heart hurt. He needs a plan and he needs it fast.

Mollie Mae Darling is about to lose everything. First her beloved grandfather and now she's just learned that the ranch she loves is about to belong to the bank. In a fateful moment she meets a handsome, sympathetic cowboy and unexpected sparks flame to life inside of her hurting heart. But she's suspicious when he makes her a crazy offer of marriage in exchange for the money she needs to keep her dream alive.

Can this be for real?

Her heart says yes, but that makes his offer all the more dangerous.

Is this the blessing she's needed for so very long?

McCoy Billionaire Brothers series...Two Billionaire Brothers determined to marry off their grandchildren...one is going to do it from the grave using his last will and testament...can the other do it before it's too late!

HER BILLIONAIRE COWBOY'S INCONVENIENT MARRIAGE BLESSING

McCoy Billionaire Brothers, Book Seven

HOPE
MOORE

Her Billionaire Cowboy's
Inconvenient Marriage Blessing
Copyright © 2020 Hope Moore

CHAPTER ONE

Beck McCoy sat at a table near the edge of the dance floor at Gruene Hall. The nostalgia of the historic first dance hall in Texas settled in around him, and some of the tension he'd felt all day eased.

Earlier today, he'd flown his Learjet into Stonewall to celebrate his sister Caroline's wedding. She'd been married for almost two months, but they were just now having the reception. He'd been surprised to learn she and Jesse, her husband, had fallen in love and were actually celebrating their marriage for real and not pretending, as they would have been doing if they'd had the reception right after the wedding.

How Granddaddy had pulled this off again was a

mystery to Beck.

Frustrated, and with a lot on his mind about the upcoming meeting that he was certain he was soon to be summoned to in the near future, Beck had come to the dance hall for a distraction. Good music and to disappear in a happy crowd seemed a better place to be than hiding out at his house on the ranch.

He had spent many of his young adult weekends right here, listening to famous singers who came to the little town of Gruene, including the great George Strait, who had gotten his start right here in the dance hall. Tonight, the new band was good, worth the hour drive from the ranch. He relaxed against his chair and watched the dancers as they all did a line dance together, looking as if they didn't have a care in the world.

That wasn't him tonight.

His gaze suddenly focused in on a pretty blonde who he realized was watching him from a table in the corner across the room. The dancers moved in front of her, then parted again as the line dance switched directions, and he realized she was still watching him.

She was pretty. As he took a sip of his drink, she stood, smoothed her skirt, and then walked around the edge of the dancers. From where he sat, she looked a little bit nervous, he thought. She was average height, with blonde hair that contrasted against her tanned skin. As he watched her, he realized she was coming over to his table.

Interesting. He wasn't sad to have something else to focus on other than his troubles. He set his drink down, looped a thumb in the pocket of his jeans, and watched her from beneath his black Stetson as she weaved through the last few people between them.

Looking really nervous, she approached him. "Hi." Her husky voice had a noticeable Texas twang that fit her wholesome appearance. "I'm Mollie Mae Darling and I noticed that you haven't been dancing. And I, well, I was wondering if you might want to? Dance. With me."

She was pretty, definitely nervous, but, he thought with admiration, courageous in coming over and asking him to dance. He figured for somebody nervous like she was that approaching a man and asking him to dance was a big deal.

But he wondered why she picked him; there were other guys standing around, not dancing. With a quick glance around, he could see they were all wondering the same thing as several single guys watched her with open interest.

"Mollie Mae, it's nice to meet you. I'm Beck." He didn't give his last name. He didn't do that much these days. He'd had a few too many women interested in him only because of his last name. "I hadn't really planned on dancing."

Uncertainty came into her pretty bluebonnet-colored eyes. "That's okay. I didn't come here to dance, anyway. I had a lot on my mind tonight and needed to be around people. You know, some mindless entertainment watching others dance to good country music."

He instantly felt bad. "Since you walked all the way over here, I think I'd like to dance after all. I'm just curious why you picked me when I can see you've got a lot of admirers who are wishing you had picked them." He hitched his brow toward all the guys watching her.

She didn't even turn her head. "Not sure either, except you look kind of like you needed a little distraction too."

That sounded just like what he had done. He didn't tell her that, though. "So, I look bored?"

She smiled, a little crooked smile that showed some pretty white teeth. "You looked about as deep in thought as I was, and I just thought maybe it'd take your mind off whatever you were thinking about, too."

The song ended behind her and the band started to play a slow song. "You know, you might be right about that. So how about we get out there and continue this conversation on the dance floor?"

"That sounds perfect. I hope you don't think I'm too forward."

He chuckled. "Um, I wouldn't classify what you just did as forward. You were very polite, and a little bit hesitant." He held his hand out to her, and she placed her hand in his. He led her to the dance floor and then slid his free hand around her waist and tugged her close, but not too close. He kept his body separate from hers, but that didn't stop him from getting a whiff of her soft floral shampoo as her blonde hair tickled his nose and tempted him more than he'd been tempted in too long to count. He inhaled and tugged her so their bodies brushed each other, just close enough without stepping across the line. She'd been absolutely right; she was definitely distracting.

The song, an old one in tribute to the late, great, Kenny Rogers, was pure old country. "Lucille" was a good song to dance to. But it was also one of his granddaddy's favorites. The instant thoughts of Granddaddy moved into his head, Beck shoved them out, really not wanting to think of his granddaddy right now. Not when he had this pretty, blue-eyed woman in his arms.

Her gaze locked onto his as they moved together to the music. She was a good dancer; she followed his lead well and when she looked up at him, all thoughts of his granddaddy evaporated at the sadness that stole into her eyes.

"Is something wrong?" he asked.

She gave a sad smile. "My granddaddy loved this

song."

Okay, that was too familiar-sounding. "Really? I was just thinking that my granddaddy loves this song. It is a good one."

She looked sad. "Written in their era. It's kind of appropriate that they're playing his song. Especially the first song I dance to tonight. I came here tonight with him on my mind."

He guided them through the crowd, and she two-stepped smoothly with him. "I sense some sadness there. You say your granddaddy loved this, past tense. Did he pass away?"

She looked back up at him. "Yes, four days ago. He raised me, so it's been tough. Which makes it all the more weird that I came to the dance hall, right after I lost my granddaddy. But he loved this place. He used to come here as a young man. I just thought it would be a nice place to come and sit for a while."

Beck's heart hurt for her. "I'm sorry for your loss. My granddaddy also came here as a young man. He's still alive, though. Thankfully." Just thinking about his granddaddy dying made his gut hurt and his heart ache.

As mad as he was at his granddaddy right now, the thought of losing him just cut too deep. Especially when they were about to be at extreme odds with each other.

"That's a blessing." Her words were soft and her gaze sincere.

He continued to lead them through the crowd, shifting his gaze away from her. The thought of him and his granddaddy being torn apart by his granddaddy's eccentric ideas this late in his granddaddy's life was hard. And something Beck didn't want to think about but was being forced to face. Because there was no way to get around their soon-to-happen fallout. Granddaddy wouldn't back down and neither would he.

It was a tough situation and he resented that his granddaddy was forcing his hand on this. He resented it like nothing he'd ever resented in his life...well, other than the fact that both of his parents had been killed in that plane crash when he was young. Yeah, he'd resented that.

"Are you okay?" She looked up at him with

concern.

Her question brought him back from his thoughts. He paused their dance steps and she bumped into him. He looked into her eyes. He wasn't the one who'd lost a loved one—she was, and yet she was asking whether he was okay. "I'm fine. The question is, are you?"

Tears formed in her eyes and he saw she'd been barely holding up. She was in mourning and it was easy to see.

"Not really," she whispered.

"Would you want to go outside for some fresh air?" Every instinct in him told him not to get involved in her business, to step away from her. But he was drawn to her. And he couldn't help himself.

She nodded. "That might be good. I'll get hold of myself. I've had a wave of sadness and I'd hate to start bawling in here with people all around."

He gave her a reassuring smile. "Come on." Holding her hand, he led her through the crowd and out the side door. The small town of Gruene was a busy place on the weekends. Cars across the way filled the parking lot because the gristmill and dance hall were popular places. He looked around and found a spot under the tree with a bench.

He led her to the bench, realizing he was still holding her hand. It felt good and she seemed to need the comfort, so he didn't pull away. "Want to sit and talk?"

She looked pensive but nodded. "That sounds good. Thanks."

She had pulled her hand away as she sat down and he had a sense of sadness. That was strange. He had just met her, so why he was feeling sad, he didn't know.

"It's a nice night." Music drifted to them from inside and he gave her time to lead the conversation. It was her choice.

She bit her lip and let her gaze slide away from his as she looked around. "Yes, it is. I'm glad I came here. I'd just be sitting at the ranch, worrying, if I hadn't come."

He sat and leaned back on the bench seat, popped his boots out in front of him, crossed his ankles, pushed his Stetson back a little bit, and looked at her.

"You really do seem worried about something. Is this more than just your granddaddy dying? Which is a terrible thing...but I'm sensing as much worry from you as grief. Were you and your granddaddy having a hard patch when he died? I'm not prepared for my granddaddy to die, I can tell you that. We're having a little bit of a troubling situation between us right now, and I'd hate for something to happen to him in the midst of all of that. It worries me." *Why had he told her that?*

She swallowed hard. "Well, me and my granddaddy, we weren't having a hard time between us. I'm sad that you and your granddaddy are." She bit her lip again.

He realized it must be a nervous habit but it sure did draw his attention to her pretty lips.

"We buried my granddaddy two days ago but it's the will we went over today that has me lost."

"Something bad in it?" He felt weird asking about her personal business, but she seemed as if she needed to talk about it with someone, and he wouldn't betray her trust. If she trusted him enough to use him as a sounding board.

She sat on her hands, leaning one way and then the other as she slipped one hand under each thigh. Her stirring around sent that soft floral scent of hers his way. He fought off the wild urge to lean in her direction. He hadn't ever reacted to the scent of a woman like that.

"My granddaddy owns some land. A small ranch that I grew up on. And, well, I've always worked it. I was all he had, and it was just me and him. We were able to make a living, the two of us, with the cattle. Well, there's a…never mind…but my granddaddy, I told him many times that I would go get a job somewhere else. I have a degree in teaching—I can go be a schoolteacher. But he always told me no; he needed me at the ranch. He liked us working together. He was lonely after my grandma died, and I hated to leave him. So, I stayed. And now, I find out that my granddaddy hasn't paid the taxes and I'm going to lose the ranch. He lied to me. I never thought that he would not tell me the truth."

He cringed inside for her. "Maybe he was trying to

protect you."

"Maybe. But I could have helped. All this time, he's been paying me to stay at the ranch to work when I could have been working somewhere else. I knew that when we sold cows that it wasn't always what he'd hoped. But he always said everything was fine and that the money he'd been paid from the oil company to lease the land while they looked for oil was good. That it helped us out. I didn't know that he was not telling the truth about that, too. I didn't dig into his personal files. My granddaddy had always had a good mind. The fact that he'd started forgetting a few things was no reason for me to think he had dementia. I mean, I forget things sometimes. But I was in denial, I guess, because he was making bad decisions and I didn't intervene."

"Bad decisions? What kind?"

She sighed. "First, he insisted on paying me to work on the ranch rather than me going out and getting a job somewhere else. Granddaddy must have been lonelier after Grandmother passed away than I thought, because that's the only reason I can think of that he would make such a bad business decision. It's terrible. The bank is about to repossess it." She looked at him, tears in her eyes. "I'm sorry, I really am. I never should have started talking to you about this. I should have just sat over there at my table and kept to myself."

She seemed so alone. They weren't sitting that far apart, and he couldn't help himself; he placed his arm around her shoulders and gently pulled her against him. She laid her head on his shoulder as her shoulders shook. His heart ached for her and he just tried to give her support as she wept silently.

After a few minutes, looking embarrassed, she sat back up. "I'm so sorry. I truly am. But it was just me and my granddaddy, and my granddaddy was a hard man. People didn't really understand him because he was kind of a hermit. That was another reason why I stayed. I loved him with all my heart but he kind of ran off all his friends through the years and, to be honest, there was just nobody to talk to. Maybe that's why I came here tonight, just because I needed to be around people since…there wasn't anybody at his funeral. I just held a small ceremony at the gravesite for him."

He thought *he* had troubles. He thought about all of his family, about how close they all were, and then all of his friends. He knew he was blessed but now he had a deeper appreciation.

"But what about your friends? Don't you have some? Didn't any of them show up?"

She swiped at her cheeks, wiping away the dampness. "I do. But, I've been working so hard, I had let most of them go by the wayside. It happened little by little and when Granddaddy died, I realized it had been a couple of years since I'd even called any of my old friends.

"I hadn't meant to distance myself but a little bit at a time, I'd done it. You know, turning down invitations to lunch over and over again sends the wrong signals and eventually people stop calling. And my closest friend moved to Minnesota several years ago, and we've just drifted apart. I'd really isolated myself and didn't realize how much until the funeral."

"I guess that's easy to do. So, what are you going to do?"

She looked away. She looked pale in the light. "I guess I'm going to let the bank take it. I have until the end of the month. But it's a lot of money. It's not a big ranch, by Texas standards, but it's seven hundred acres. Some of that is a large ravine that cuts through one side, which cuts out a lot of usable land. But I'd say it's at least six hundred usable acres. I can't come up with the back taxes on it because its way too much. I'm a sixth-generation Texan. My family came to this land in a covered wagon. And now I'm letting the bank have it. It's horrible. I feel like I'm letting down generations of family. It's the hardest thing I've ever done, other than bury my granddaddy and grandmother. That ranch is the only place I've ever known as my home. I never knew my mom and dad. He ran off before I was born, and my mother died giving birth to me, so it was just me and my grandparents." She wiped at the tears.

"You've had a rough time of it." She wouldn't look at him and he knew she was embarrassed.

"I really wish I hadn't told you this." She shook her head and her brows knitted over conflicted eyes.

"It sounds like something I read in a romance novel where the heroine has nobody. But that's my life." She slid him an apologetic look. "I'm sure you don't read romances, so you have no idea what I'm talking about."

"Not a romance reader." He had released her when she'd sat up, but he'd kept his arm on the back of the bench. Now he fought the urge to pull her against him again and tell her everything would be okay. "Still, I'm sorry you have all of this on your shoulders."

"Me too. But my granddaddy didn't raise me to be a crybaby, so I'll pull up my big-girl panties, after this moment of weakness here with you, and I'll do what I have to do. Thank you so much for listening, giving me a place to voice my woes. Now, I just have to face reality. I still have my health and I'm young. I can start over, right?"

"Yes." He nodded, knowing what that felt like himself.

"It's late and I've got about a thirty-minute drive to the outskirts of Blanco. So, I'll say goodnight. And thank you." She stood.

"Are you sure you're okay?" He wasn't ready for her to leave. He wanted to pull her back into his arms. That wouldn't help her situation at all—the guy she just met at the dance hall trying to hug on her. And he was so tempted to kiss her—which was so terribly inappropriate that it embarrassed him. He stepped back. He was so mixed up himself over his own granddaddy that probably the best thing he could do was let her go home.

She nodded. "I love the ranch dearly. It's my little piece of heaven, and I always thought it would be mine. But I'll be fine."

He hated this. "Look, I'm really sorry about what's going on in your life right now. I don't really know what else to say to you, but I wish you all the luck in the world. Don't give up yet. Talk to the bank and tell them your situation. Maybe the bank will work with you."

She pushed her shoulders back and he thought she was trying to look strong. "I already called them. But I might do it again. I'm a pretty strong person, I guess tonight's my night to have a weak moment." Her eyes grew misted as she took his hand. "Thank you for being there for me."

He couldn't help himself; he pulled her forward and wrapped his arms around her. She could use a hug more than anyone he knew right now. He breathed in the scent of her as she settled in against him, as if giving in to the need for another hug in that minute. "You take care of yourself, Mollie Mae Talbot. Maybe you give that friend of yours a call. I'm sure she would be glad to give you a little support."

She nodded, and then he let go of her and she stepped back. It was hard letting her go. It startled him that it was so hard. She smiled at him, and then she turned and walked away.

He watched her and, for a crazy moment, he wanted to run after her. Beck had never run after anybody in his life. He told himself it was just because of her situation.

He stood there for a long time and then, he headed to the parking lot, toward his own truck. It was time to go home. He had his own demons to face tomorrow. His phone had vibrated earlier, and he had a feeling he knew who it was.

He pulled his phone out of his pocket and looked at the text message. Just as he'd thought, it was from Granddaddy.

He was calling a family meeting first thing in the morning. And for Beck, that meant his time was up. It was time to face the music.

CHAPTER TWO

Beck drove up to the barn of his granddaddy's big stone house. He was still thinking about Mollie this morning, having had her on his mind even after the summons from Granddaddy.

Meeting Mollie Mae had given him some relief from his own worries of losing his charter plane company because his granddaddy had pretty much gone off the deep end over the last year. Mollie was losing her heritage because her granddaddy hadn't been able to pay his taxes. Beck was losing his successful business because his granddaddy wanted to control Beck's life, and Beck wasn't going to allow it. He was going to walk away.

His brothers waited for him on the porch. They'd

both tried to talk him into taking the deal. It had worked out for both of them, and their sister and their cousins. But it was the principle of it all that had Beck riled up. He wasn't in the surrendering kind of mood. Feeling ornery, he climbed from his truck.

Denton, looking every bit the country singing sensation that he'd become, wore his Stetson low over his eyes as he watched Beck approach. "I was beginning to think you were going to be a no-show."

"I'm here."

"Good." Ash clamped a hand to his shoulder. "Promise me you are not going to do anything you'll regret. Give it some time and see what happens."

"I'm not making any promises," Beck said.

Ash frowned. "You don't need to just throw your inheritance away when you go in there this morning. Me and Denton and Caroline—we all know that you're not going to put up with it. I know, we all said the same thing and then somehow, we were each blessed in ways we never even dreamed of. It could happen to you. You should at least give this a shot."

Denton's lip hitched. "There's something going on

around here and it's good."

"Find someone you could bless with this situation."

Bless?

"Fellas, I know things turned out well for you both, but I don't want to do what y'all did. I don't want to give Granddaddy that satisfaction."

Denton looked exasperated. "Listen to Ash. Don't make a rash decision. You have worked your rear off to make your private jet charter business a success. Don't give it up just because you're mad."

He stared at his brothers, inhaled, and counted to ten. They were doing this out of love; they were just trying to talk sense into him. All through their lives, the three brothers had talked one another off ledges at one time or another.

"I'm not making any promises." He reached for the door, ready to get this over with now.

Grim-faced, his brothers didn't say anything else, but he knew they weren't happy with him as they followed him into the house and down the hallway to Granddaddy's office.

He walked into the office. The scent of leather and freshly polished wood greeted them. Caroline smiled from where she sat in a chair near the window. She could see everyone's face from that vantage point, he noted. She was probably going to try to smooth the way, knowing Caroline.

"Good morning, brothers. Beck, don't look like a sour puss. You may be about to find your one true love. Something's in the water."

He glared at her. "Caroline, sometimes you talk too much."

She laughed. "I won't say that's not true."

Knowing Granddaddy was watching him, Beck strode to stand near the fireplace, where he always stood during these meetings. He propped an elbow on the mantel and knocked his hat back with the thumb of his hand. Only then did he speak to his granddaddy. "I'm here."

"So you are." Granddaddy smiled as Denton took a chair in front of the big desk and Ash sat in a chair across from Caroline.

There was one chair left in the room and it was the

one next to Denton, across from his granddaddy's desk. Beck wasn't sitting in it. He just waited. Tension in the room sizzled as his brothers and his sister watched the locked horns of him and his granddaddy.

Talbert McCoy laid his hands out wide on his desk. "I'm not going to talk long this morning. Y'all know why we're here. Beck, I saved you for last because I knew you were going to be like this. And I was hoping if you saw positive things happen in your cousins' lives and your brothers' and your sister's lives that you would be more open to this. The last thing I want is for you to walk away and not even attempt to find a wife. I don't want you to just give up all you've worked so hard for with your charter business. But business isn't everything. Love is what makes this world go around. And you need to figure that out. As you know, I own a slight majority of stock in your company since a couple of your shareholders sold out to me a while back."

Yes, he knew it. "Of course, I know it. And this is how I assumed this was going to go."

"No sense beating around the bush and give you

more time to swell up at me anymore. When you walk out the door, you have three months to find a wife and you have to stay married for three months. Or I take control of your McCoy Flight Charters."

Beck seethed. "It doesn't matter if you give me a day or three months. I'm not taking you up on your ridiculous takeover of my business. If you're going to do it, then do it." He started for the door.

Granddaddy stood. "I knew you were going to say that. But I'm giving you the time anyway. I'm not taking your company until at least the end of my conditions. I love you and I'm just wanting you to have an open mind. Don't you want a wife and family of your own?"

Beck halted at the door. He snatched his Stetson from his head and spun toward the man he loved with all his heart. And whom he no longer understood. "Granddaddy, maybe I do and maybe I don't, but it's up to me. It is not up to you when and if I choose a wife."

"And that's your choice. I made promises that I would make sure you and your brothers and sister lived happy lives. So, your time starts now, when you walk out that door. And I'm prepared to take extra steps in this challenge, so you'll find a wife, if I have to."

"Challenge? Is that how you're looking at this? If so, I'm not taking the challenge. I'm leaving it all on the table and I'll start new. You can hire a manager and enjoy my business."

Granddaddy hitched a brow, his gaze drilling into him and unease seeped into Beck's gut. *What was his granddaddy up to?*

Talbert leaned back in his chair. "So you're taking the easy way out and forgoing taking the actual challenge—finding a wife, most likely a stranger, and staying married for three months is the hard way. I'm challenging you to do it the hard way."

His granddaddy knew what made Beck tick...he'd never met a challenge he couldn't win if he set his mind to it.

This was different.

This time he was walking away.

Without another word, Beck turned and walked out the door. He needed fresh air. He needed to go back to his corner of the ranch, get his horse out and ride. He did his best thinking flying in the sky or flying across the ranch on the fastest horse he owned.

Today, he needed to feel the hooves of the horse pounding out his frustrations as it galloped across the ranch he loved.

The ranch he would also be walking away from soon.

CHAPTER THREE

Mollie wiped her sweaty brow with the back of her arm and then reached for the barbed-wire fence she was repairing. Her leather gloves held tight as she twisted the ends of the barbed wire together, a cheap, temporary fix to the busted fence. Hopefully this would prevent any more calves from getting out on the country road and causing an accident.

Done, she shook her head, staring at the repair. "Why are you fixing this?" she asked out loud. The bank basically owned it now. *This and all your hard work was going down the drain.* So why put any more of her sweat and tears into the place?

Her heart squeezed hard and tears burned in the back of her eyes.

This was all she knew. Taking care of this falling-apart ranch. It might not be much but she took pride in that she'd worked hard here and knew how to keep things running. Her granddaddy might not have thought enough of her to tell her the truth, but she wasn't stupid; she could've handled it. If he'd told her how bad things were, she could have helped.

Salty, angry tears streamed down her face. *Why had this happened?*

Here, alone in the wide-open space, the sun beaming down on her, the anger radiated from her. This was her place as much as it was her granddaddy's. She'd poured her life into this beloved land and now it was being taken away from her. She yanked her gloves off, threw them on the ground, and wiped the tears off her face. *She was not going to cry.*

Crying did not solve anything.

She had learned that a long time ago. No, she didn't have long to save the place but she wasn't giving up yet. Maybe there was something she could do…if she found a job and showed the bank she had a job and could make payments, maybe they'd let her keep the ranch and pay off the back taxes.

The fact that she had never actually gotten a loan for anything wasn't helpful. She was twenty-five and clueless.

Her car had been her grandmother's, so she'd never even borrowed money to buy a car. Nope, she'd basically just let the world float on by while she stayed out here and worked the ranch with Granddaddy. Sniffing, she wiped her damp nose with the sleeve of her shirt. She bent down and picked up her gloves, then trudged back toward the ancient pickup truck that had been Granddaddy's. She had told him many times that he needed to buy a new truck and he had told her he liked his truck; it was a classic and he didn't want to give it up. Now she understood completely—he hadn't been able to afford a better truck.

So many things he had told her had been lies. "Granddaddy, I swear, if you were here, I'd give you a piece of my mind!" She yelled the words so loud she startled several cows. "You did bad. You did really bad." Guilt struck her, knowing that her granddaddy had gotten forgetful. But had it been bad enough for him to forget to tell her how bad a fix the ranch was in?

She thought not. He'd been lonely and wanted her to be here for him. And he'd paid her a salary instead of the taxes.

Anger building to the level of explosion, she climbed behind the wheel and cranked the engine. It sputtered to life, thankfully. It did have a good engine. That was good because it was going to get her where she needed to go. She was going to sell her car for the cash. After they took the ranch, she was going to need a little cash for a new start.

As she drove up to the ranch house, every detail that needed to be repaired suddenly jumped out at her. She'd just gotten used to how things looked. All she cared about was working the cows, keeping the fences up, and selling the cows when the time came. Thinking all the time that she was keeping the ranch afloat by doing her job.

What a joke. All the time, it wasn't enough. Nothing she had done was enough. She sat in the truck and eyed the house. Her thoughts went back to last night when she had sat there in that dance hall, sulking.

Her gaze had caught on that good-looking cowboy and she had done something she had never done in her life when she'd walked over and asked him to dance. It was a sure act of desperation, was what it was. She'd realized she was going to fall to pieces if she didn't do something and dancing seemed like a good thing to do. And, for a little while, as he held her in his arms, everything in the world had been right.

Then it had all fallen apart; the tears had ambushed her and then she'd told him too much. It felt weird and she felt very self-conscious, having exposed her soul to a practical stranger.

Getting out of the truck, she stormed up to the house. It was time to quit crying and go see if she could find a job. It was a long shot, but it was all she had—she was going to try to talk the bank president into letting her keep this ranch.

She wasn't going to lose it without a fight.

* * *

Beck rode hard and fast across the pasture. Laramie, his stallion, loved when he came home and gave the horse his way and let him race. Today, Beck let the horse plow across that land. He had lost his hat back behind him somewhere along the way and hadn't worried about it. The stallion had felt his frustration and flew, as if it knew that speed and wind in their faces and the pounding of his hooves would help.

It had. At least, while it lasted.

When they reached the river, Beck dismounted, dropped the reins, and let Laramie take his fill of the water. Beck strode to the river's edge, watching the rushing water as his thoughts churned. Instead of his thoughts going back to what his granddaddy was trying to force him to do, his thoughts went to Mollie Mae Talbot.

She'd constantly been coming back and forth into his thoughts. She had looked so desperate, so alone last night. Mollie, from the sound of it, didn't have anybody. And then, the one person she thought had her back, her granddaddy, had died and left her a mess. She probably felt like the ranch was all she had left of her family and the bank was taking it. This ranch meant a lot to him. Before he'd been killed in the plane crash, Beck's daddy had taught him to love this ranch.

And then his granddaddy had taken the reins and continued to teach him to love the land. *You always had the land to fall back on*, was their motto. His heart clenched. That was obviously not the case for him or for Mollie.

"Figure out somebody you can bless."

Ash's words hit Beck and suddenly he was alert. *Could he do that?*

Did he want *to do that?*

He wondered how she would feel about a crazy scheme to join up with him, to come out of it with her ranch paid off—lock, stock, and barrel—and cash in her bank account.

And him walking away with his inheritance and his charter plane fleet.

He barely knew her and had a feeling she would probably look at him like he was loco. Which he was, if he were even considering this. But she needed help.

The timing was strange that she would show up on the eve of his verdict coming down from Granddaddy. Maybe God was sending him a sign that he could help somebody.

Lost in thought and restless, he took the reins in his hand once more and in one easy motion, he swung up into the saddle. "Time to head back. Time to shut this pity party down and take action." With a simple nudge from his knee, the horse reared onto his back legs and his hooves pawed in the air.

Beck grinned. "I know exactly how you feel. Go for it." And with that, the horse's hooves hit the ground and he took off like a shot, back the way they'd come.

It was time to go home.

* * *

"Yes, ma'am. I understand. I haven't ever been a waitress, but I'm willing to try. And to do my best." Mollie smiled at the lady who owned the café. She was a small lady with brown hair piled on top of her head in an old-fashioned bun. She wore a pink dress with a white apron and a name tag that said Dixie. Now, her bright-red lipstick lips widened into a smile.

Though Mollie didn't come this way often, she'd spent the afternoon driving around, looking for a job. At the diner in Blanco, one of the waitresses told her that Dixie's in Stonewall had just lost one of her waitresses and that it was a pretty busy little café and she would make good tips. Without hesitating, Mollie had driven the short distance and was now biting her lip nervously as Dixie studied her with keen eyes. She was being measured up. She tried not to look like she was pleading; she just tried to look competent and she gave Dixie a little smile. "I promise, I will work really hard. And I really need the job."

"Well hon, you look nice and my customers would like your smiling face, so you can have this job."

"Thank you!" Mollie almost threw her arms around her new boss but caught herself before she launched herself at the poor woman.

Dixie grinned. "Glad to see your enthusiasm. I hope you don't fall in love right away. I do have some hunky cowboys who enjoy my cooking. I'm thinking you won't last long."

"I promise I won't fall in love. You must lose a lot of waitresses to love?"

Dixie rolled her eyeballs. "I lose more waitresses to cowboys than I can count. Claire was different, or so I thought. However, the minute that young man walked in here and they locked eyes, I saw the writing on the wall. It was only a matter of time. But I'd thought she was immune because she'd never even acted attracted to any of the McCoy men. And that's a big test because up until a few months ago, they were all available but didn't take the thought of marriage seriously. They're the catches of the county. Then, out of the blue, J.D. McCoy died right there in that booth, eating a piece of my pecan pie—not my pie's fault, I assure you. No, the good Lord just called his number in that moment. Then, the strangest thing happened...his three grandsons all got married, one right after the other, and then his brother Talbert's grandsons and his granddaughter got married, too. Now all those single McCoys are married...all but one. And he's a dreamboat...well, I'll be." Her eyes widened. "He's parking his truck now.

"We'll see how you fare against all that gorgeousness. And money—they've got more money than they know what to do with. But you didn't hear me say that. A good waitress takes things in but doesn't repeat it, ya hear?"

"Yes, ma'am."

"Now, you tell me if what I saw ain't the truth after you wait on him. Here, you just hand him this menu." She grabbed a menu from the rack on the wall and slapped it into Mollie's hands.

Mollie was shocked as she looked down at the laminated sheet, then back up at Dixie. "But I don't know what to do."

"You smile that pretty smile of yours and you welcome him and then seat him in one of the booths. Then you hand him that and ask him what you can get for him. He knows what he likes. I'll be back here cooking, since Jude is off today. I was fixin' to be in a real fix until you walked in the door. It's not fun waiting tables and playing cook too. Thankfully, it was just for the slow hours."

Mollie watched her hurry to the back and then Mollie spun to look at the door just as it opened. She dropped the menu the moment she saw the hunky McCoy walk in the door.

It was Beck. Her cowboy from last night. The one she'd danced with…the one she hadn't been able to stop thinking about.

CHAPTER FOUR

Beck walked into Dixie's Diner and stopped when he saw Mollie Mae Talbot standing in the middle of the diner, looking at him with wide eyes.

He yanked his hat off his head. "Well, hey, fancy meeting you here."

She blushed. "Hi. I can't believe you're the first person I see."

This really was weird. He'd never seen her before and now, to run into her twice in a row… He stopped by on a whim, after leaving his granddaddy's, thinking some pancakes might soothe his temper. He'd known this would be the mid-morning slump and the place might be less crowded. He hadn't thought it would be empty—or that Mollie would be here.

"Did you come in here to get something to eat?"

"Actually, I was looking for a job and heard Dixie was hiring, so I drove over and got the job. I've never waitressed but I'm going to give it my all." She gave a weak smile. "I decided not to just lay down and not give the bank my ranch. I decided to at least fight for it."

"Good for you."

"Thanks. To do that, I need a job and quite honestly, I'm scared to death. Dixie is taking a chance on me." She waved at Dixie, who peeped through the pass-through from the kitchen.

"Hey there, you handsome cowboy," Dixie called and waved at him. "Have a seat."

"Oh, yes, let me show you to a booth. Sorry." Mollie picked up a menu from the floor and led him to a booth.

He smiled. "It's fine."

"I heard Claire ran off with a cowboy."

"Yes, she did," Dixie called from the back. The woman had ears like an elephant. "You cowboys need to leave my waitresses alone."

He laughed. "Yes, ma'am. I'm not the guilty one, so please don't burn my pancakes."

"You know I would never do such a thing. But I'm glad to see you two know each other. That's real nice."

"Yes, it is." He winked at Mollie. "So, wow, this really is a coincidence."

"Yes." She hugged the menu to her and smiled at him. "A nice one for me. I wasn't expecting to ever see you again. I didn't even know your last name. And I just want to say I'm really embarrassed about last night. But you were so kind to me, and I thank you from the bottom of my heart."

"It's McCoy. I'm sorry I never got around to telling you my whole name. I was glad to be there for you." They stared at each other. A lot of thoughts churned through his head as he stared at her, still so stunned to see her.

"I didn't just mean to lay all my troubles out to you like that. I swear, sometimes when I'm upset, I just talk too much. And I'm not really a crier, I promise. It actually takes a lot for me to cry, so that was just even more embarrassing to me that I broke down. And you had to witness all that, when you had just come out there for a good night, a good time—and some crazy woman just came up and messed up your night." She waved the menu as her exasperation had mounted and then, as if realizing she'd never given it to him, she laid it down in front of him.

On impulse, he laid his hand on her arm before she pulled it away. "Mollie, you don't have anything to apologize for. I'm really glad I was there to give you some kind of support. And I'm very glad you're going to fight for your property." His hand slid gently down her arm and rested on her hand. He told himself it was for comfort, but he realized he just wanted to touch her. "I'm wishing you all the luck. Maybe since you got a job, the bank will give you an extension and stop the foreclosure."

She nodded and he saw her swallow hard. He gently rubbed his thumb on the soft skin of her wrist, trying to figure out the right thing to say. "If you are here or you do a really good job, which I'm sure you will, I know Dixie will give you a good reference if you ask her." Reluctantly, he pulled his hand away from her and fingered the menu when she straightened and leaned a thigh against the table.

"That would be great. I'll ask her. To be honest, Beck, I've never gotten a loan before. Granddaddy bought my car—well, it was my grandmother's before she passed—and I never had a reason to get any other kind of loan, so it's a little bit nerve-racking." She inhaled, as if trying to steady her breathing.

He wanted with all his heart to help her calm down; however, it seemed like he was only making her situation worse by talking about it. He picked up the menu and stared at it, even though he knew he was going to have a breakfast plate with a side of pancakes. He loved Dixie's breakfast. The woman could cook eggs better than anybody and her pancakes were like heaven on a plate. "I'll just have the breakfast special. And some coffee, please, and some water, too."

She looked startled then she blushed again. "I am so sorry. See, there I went again, just talking about my troubles instead of taking your order like I was supposed to. I'll go tell Dixie this is what you want, and I'll bring your drinks out in just a second." She spun and practically ran to the window at the end of the diner.

Beck watched her and his thoughts churned. Mollie returned with a cup of hot coffee and a glass of ice water.

She set them on the table in front of him then took a step back. "Would you like some cream and sugar with that? I guess I should have asked. I'm going to get better. I promise."

She was cute. "I drink it black but thank you. And relax. The folks who come here are nice, salt-of-the-earth folks and will love having you wait on them. Just be your nice self and you'll do fine. Everybody will love you. You just smile that pretty smile of yours and be helpful, and nobody will give you a hard time."

Her smile widened. "Thanks. In all honesty, yesterday I was out fixing barbed-wire fences. I should be happy that I won't have to do that any longer. I'm going to look on the bright side and believe that something good is going to come from all of this. Being in town, at least maybe I'll make some new friends and renew old friendships. Since Granddaddy's been gone, it is terribly lonely out there by myself. I'll need this job to help myself find an apartment or somewhere to live, *if* I can't save the ranch. Okay, sorry, I'm talking about my troubles again." She blushed really red this time. "I'm going to go now and wait on your order and let you sit here in peace."

He frowned. "There's nobody in here and I like talking to you."

She looked like she wasn't sure whether she should go or stay. "Well, if you're sure. I like talking to you too, but I didn't want to be a bother."

"You're no bother. I enjoy your company." It was true, he realized.

Something about Mollie calmed him, made him smile. And after yesterday, that was a really good thing.

* * *

Mollie worked the morning through the afternoon shift for the next three days. Beck had been right:

everybody who had come in was extremely nice and helpful and though she messed up a few orders, she was turning out to be a fairly decent waitress. Oh, she couldn't carry a bunch of plates at one time like she had seen the older waitress Peg doing, but Dixie and Peg both told her if she lasted that long, she'd be able to do it. She hadn't seen Beck again and she'd been disappointed about that. It had been twice she got to meet him and twice she probably ran him off. She'd be lucky if he ever came back in there again, she blabbered so much, talking about her troubles.

Why did she keep doing that? Especially after learning how wealthy the McCoys were? It was the bank she needed to be talking to, not spilling her guts to Beck. But she had a plan. She wanted to work at least five days before asking Dixie for a reference. She needed a good—or better yet, a glowing—reference if she wanted anything from the bank.

She hadn't been able to get Beck off her mind. He never really told her anything about himself but she was familiar with the McCoy family name. They were a well-known family in these parts. Wealthy beyond anything she'd ever imagine, and yet you would never know it by how down-to-earth and kind Beck was. He had never said anything about the family wealth and that could have been because she had talked about being broke so much.

He was out of her league, so what was she thinking anyway? Her nerves were just getting to her, she thought as she parked her truck next to the house after work. She was glad to have Monday off. She planned to take care of a lot of things on Monday: go to the bank, and then sell her car and get some cash so she'd have the money to rent an apartment somewhere, if needed.

Today, some of the older ladies, including Miss Penny, had come in the diner for their weekly get-together. This was their second time since she'd been there and Dixie told her it was because they were sizing her up and probably going to try to find her a date. Not that Dixie wanted them doing that because she wanted her to stay around. It bothered Mollie a little bit that everybody thought that she had to have a man in her life. She didn't. And it didn't help that she had a man on her mind. One in her life and one on her mind were not the same thing.

But after she got her life straightened out, she might start looking for someone to date.

Hiding out on a ranch and working with cows all day limited a young woman on her choices. But that didn't mean that she had to have a man to make her life better. Her first paycheck was in her purse and she was proud of that slip of paper. It gave her hope that maybe the bank would pay attention to her.

She changed clothes, then fed her chickens and goats before heading to the garden. She had a large garden in the summer, and even her fall garden was good size. Her strawberries were doing great and she'd have a lot of fresh jam. She was going to have more than she'd be able to eat alone but that was nothing new. She always sold some at the farmers' market in Blanco on Saturday mornings. People loved her jams and her fresh eggs, too.

She was watering her bell peppers when the water sputtered and stopped. With a sigh, she laid the hose down and headed toward the small shack of a building that housed the water well. She hated the building and going inside. She never knew what she was going to encounter.

She'd dreamed of a new well and automatic watering system. But that was not going to happen now.

Her shoulders slumped as she pulled the creaking old door open and peered into the dilapidated shack that leaned precariously to one side. It gave her the creeps. Ignoring her fear and trepidation, she stomped her feet and took a step inside so she could reach upward for the chain dangling in the center of the building and turn on the low-watt light bulb. She shivered. This, too, had been on her list of things to fix eventually. She'd hoped many nights that a fierce Texas wind might blow it down, but so far, no such luck. She shivered, thinking about the big chicken snakes that liked to curl up on the rafters and scare years off her age.

Trying not to worry, she concentrated on the dials and valves. When the pump didn't respond, she kicked it as a last resort. It came alive then. Feeling worried, she reminded herself that this was nothing new…that the water well had been giving them issues for a long time and that it always pulled through…she went back out and finished watering her garden.

A garden that, soon, would no longer have her to water it.

That night, sitting on the porch, holding one of her baby goats, her heart was heavy. She missed her granddaddy. And soon, she would miss this place. And her goats… She loved baby goats. They were nuisances and ate everything they could get their little lips around, but they were adorable. Yes, they grew up to be ornery. But they kept her fence line nibbled down and they loved eating hats. Granddaddy had lost several hats to the goats through the years.

"I miss you, Granddaddy," she whispered into the night as she stroked the soft coat of the baby goat. Without her granddaddy, this was going to be a really lonely place.

The goat licked her cheek, drawing her out of her melancholy. "Thanks, sweetie," she whispered as a tear trickled down her cheek.

Tears again. She knew she was still grieving. And worried and stressed. So she gave herself some grace where crying was concerned. She just hoped eventually they dried up.

Looking out at the stars, her thoughts went to Beck. She wondered what he was doing. Her mind went instantly to being in his arms...a much more pleasant place to be.

She was alone way out here, so for a few minutes, she decided it wouldn't hurt to let her mind think about him.

* * *

Beck landed in Chicago. He hated this airport. He loved flying but this airport was so busy; it just bothered him. Thankfully, he got to fly into the less busy terminal with the private jets. As he let Alex, his copilot today, get off and tell their clients to have a nice day, he finished up his paperwork and then stood. He had been working and trying not to think about decisions he had to make. Thinking about walking away was pounding at his brain, giving him a constant headache. He exited the plane and walked across the tarmac to the hangar, where he got a drink out of the soda machine and checked his messages.

Denton asking him what he had decided.

Ash asking him what he had decided.

His cousin Wade asking him what he had decided.

His cousin Todd asking him what he had decided.

His cousin Morgan asking him what he had decided.

And Caroline asking him what he had decided.

Wow. Would they all stop asking? Enough already. Stuffing his phone back into his pocket, he was coming out of the men's room a few minutes later when he ran into Jack Carson. Jack owned another charter business. He liked Jack; they had always gotten along.

"Hey Beck, I'm hearing rumors that your charter business might be up for sale?"

Alarm bells went off in his brain. "What did you say?"

"That's what word is on the tarmac. I heard it

from somebody who's close friends with your granddaddy."

If his granddaddy was thinking that he was going to take this business and sell it, he had another think coming. It was one thing for his granddaddy to take his business from him, but it was altogether another thing if his granddaddy was going to sell it right out from under him. The thought just wound him up inside. "No, Jack, I think you heard wrong. My charter business is not for sale. You and I both know how hard it is to build up a business like this. I'm not selling it."

"Well, I thought it sounded off. I mean, I know he owns stock but not controlling."

Beck could barely speak and his exasperation must have shown on his face because Jack gave him a grim look. "Yeah, I know what you mean. Stockholders can be a pain in the you know what."

"You can say that again. My granddaddy's giving me a little bit of trouble. But believe me, my business is not for sale. And thanks for telling me. I've got to go—catch you next time. Next time you're in the Texas area, give me a ring and I'll try to meet you somewhere…have dinner or something."

"That'd be good. One of these days, maybe you and I need to think about joining up with a side charter or something. Who knows what we could come up with?"

He didn't tell Jack that one of his plans, if it came down to it, was seeing whether Jack needed a pilot. But right now, he kept that to himself as he stewed over what he had just learned. He was going to have a meeting of the minds with Granddaddy. He was not taking this.

CHAPTER FIVE

Feeling humiliated, Mollie left the bank.

She'd come straight back to the ranch, to work in the dirt and play with her goats. She didn't have very long before she couldn't.

He hadn't been unkind, yet he had been just a little bit condescending when he looked at her and told her that the ranch was too much for a single young woman and this was probably for the best.

What did he know about what was best for her?

She was tired of men thinking they knew what was best for her. Her granddaddy had thought he knew what was best for her and he had hidden everything from her. The banker was trying to tell her he knew what was best for her, and he didn't even know her. It was really irritating. Before she even realized she was back home, she smoothed the skirt of her dress. She had even put a dress on to go to the bank. She probably should have just worn her jeans and boots and old work shirt. Maybe he would have taken her seriously if he saw that she was a ranch hand.

She had never felt so small in all of her life.

She blinked back tears just as she heard a rumble and then a clank and then nothing. She knew that sound. Her steps were slow as she tramped across the yard to the side where the water well was. This was all she needed.

Without thinking, she didn't even look up; she walked in, reached out and yanked the string for the light. Instantly the tiny well house was bathed in light and she stared at the blasted, no-good gauges. She twisted a knob and fiddled with another and then heard the sound of a motor. *Who had driven up?* Maybe it was the mailman, who sometimes delivered mail to the doorstep if something came that was bigger than would fit in their mailbox at the end of the lane. If it was the mailman, he would leave it.

She kicked the water tank with her foot, forgetting she had on sandals, not her boots, and yelped with pain. Then, while she was jumping around, holding her foot, she looked up. A big black snake was hanging down, looking straight in her face.

She screamed loud enough to be heard at the North Pole as she stumbled out of the building and slammed straight into a hard wall of man. Strong arms came around her and held her up. She looked up into the face of Beck McCoy. Her knees went weak with relief. If he hadn't been holding her, she would have sunk to the ground. "Beck."

"What's going on? Are you hurt?"

"Snake," was all she could get out.

"Where? In there?"

She nodded furiously and then, thank goodness, got her voice back. "My water well is acting up. I kicked it with my sandal on, not my boot, and I looked up, and there was a snake hanging down right in my face. I just freaked out. I'm a wuss."

He laughed. "You are not a wuss." He clutched her closer to him.

"I am. I can't even save my ranch and the stinkin' snake can have it." The words came out on a sob.

"You're crying."

His soft words had her blinking back the tears that had started. She sniffed. "Why is it that every time you're around, I start crying?"

"You didn't cry at the diner last week."

"For once. But I'm just a wreck today."

"Come on, let's go back up to your porch there and sit down. You need to calm down. I'm going to go get that snake, okay, while you're up there, safely away from it."

Still holding her hand and with his other arm around her waist, he walked her to the front porch and up the steps, where she sank into the chair. She wiped her face on her sleeve. *No telling what this man thought of her.* And she couldn't believe she had been daydreaming or night dreaming about him the other night while she had been sitting right here on this very porch, cuddling her baby goat. She was pathetic. Baby goats were probably about the only things she would be cuddling. Never the likes of this gorgeous man.

"You stay right there and take some deep breaths. You got a hoe anywhere? Or a shovel?"

She nodded toward the house. "There's one down there by my garden."

He strode off and she just waited, defeated.

In a few minutes, he came back and sank down on the top step. "No more snake." He cocked his head and squinted at her from under his black Stetson. His gray T-shirt stretched over his chest.

"I saw you have a chicken coop full of chickens out there. He won't be bothering them either. You probably didn't need it eating up all your eggs."

"No, I didn't. Thank you."

"I'm glad I was here to help."

His expression turned serious as he studied her. And then it hit her.

"What *are* you doing here? How did you find me?"

"Well, I went to the diner and you weren't there. Dixie told me that you have Mondays off. She told me your address and told me you had been to the bank and you could probably use a friend."

"She told you that?"

"Yup, that's Dixie. She's a mother hen. She sounded worried about you. How did it go?"

She stared at him. *Should she just be up front with him? Should she tell him the truth or should she just tell him everything was fine and maybe he'd never know just how much her life was goofed up?* Moments ticked by as she contemplated her next move. But he was so nice and he had come all this way and he was so easy to talk to. She sighed. "It didn't go well. Didn't go well at all. I'm on my last leg here and the bank is going to take it."

* * *

Beck had hoped the bank would give her a chance.

He'd landed and gone to the ranch and confronted his granddaddy. And sure enough, selling his charter business was the way his granddaddy had upped the challenge. He'd known that was the thing that would get him.

He just felt driven to be here, to check on her. The

thought of her going through so much loss all by herself just didn't seem right to him. And then there was that idea that he could make an offer to her. Yeah, he could offer to marry her, and he'd pay off her ranch; he'd keep the bank away and then he'd keep his charter business.

It would be mutually beneficial to both of them. It would be an inconvenient marriage but maybe, maybe they could get a blessing out of it. The idea rolled through him like thunder. And where there was thunder, there was lightning. He waited for it to strike him but it didn't.

He didn't want to take advantage of her in her time of need. He was not that guy. But if he didn't offer, she would lose everything.

He cleared his throat. "What if I told you—I want to offer you a loan." He hadn't been able to make the offer of marriage. "Let me pay for your ranch and then you can pay me back. I know you wouldn't take my money. Even though I don't tell many people this, I can handle your loan without a problem. I'd like to do it at no interest. It'll be a business loan. You can make improvements and get this place where it can make you a living. I know you're looking at me like I'm crazy, but I'm serious. I feel like it's the least I can do for you."

"No. I couldn't do that. I mean, thank you. That's the sweetest offer I've ever heard, but no. The bank is taking it and I'll make it. You don't need to worry about me."

He reached for her hand. "Please, take the deal. It's a good deal." But he didn't take her hand; he just waited, thinking maybe she would come to her senses and take him up on it.

"Beck, that is probably the kindest offer I've ever had. But I can't take your money."

"Yes, you can. Like I said, it's a business loan. Just like the bank would give you." He was feeling a bit desperate now. He'd flubbed this.

* * *

A business loan? Mollie thought about it for a second, determined she could not take Beck's money. He looked very conflicted.

"You can take it. I promise you; it would be a winning situation for you. I think you can make this little ranch a success."

"I think I could too, but there are no guarantees. And I can't take your money, especially after I've been crying on your shoulder so many times. It's really humiliating. I bet with as much money as you have, you get people crying on your shoulder all the time. I'm going to be okay."

His lips flattened and her heart zinged with the way he stared at her, as though she spoke another language and he couldn't believe she was not taking his offer. *Did people take stuff from him all the time? No, she couldn't do that.* Even though it was tempting. "Besides, without Granddaddy here, it is kind of lonesome. And I don't know if I want to spend all my time out here by myself."

Only after she made the statement did she realize how that sounded. *Did he think she was making him a proposition?* She put a hand on her hip as she stood. "Now, don't get me wrong. That was not an invitation that I'm looking for somebody to move out here and help me. It's just, well, you know, maybe I have lived my life out here by myself with Granddaddy and I'm missing out. Maybe like the banker said, me getting an apartment in town and getting involved with life other than out here would be a good thing for somebody my age. That's what his advice was, anyway."

Beck's eyes narrowed on his handsome face. His jaw tightened and she could see the muscle there working. He crossed his arms and those muscles bulged again. The guy was in shape. It wasn't helping her situation that she kept noticing that. She noticed every little thing about him.

"All right then. I guess if you won't take my help, I can't force you. You sure you're okay?"

"I'm fine. And really, Beck, you've been so generous and kind to me. And you don't even know me. Well, that really means a lot to me. I really appreciate it, but honestly, you don't owe me anything and you don't have to come around again. I'll probably see you at the diner. But, anyway, thank you again, and I mean that from the bottom of my heart."

He just stared at her for a minute, looked as if he was going to say something else, and then he nodded. "Okay then, I'm going to go. I don't know if I'll see you at the diner the next couple of days—I've got flights, I own a charter service."

"A charter service?"

"Yeah, for private jets."

"Oh," she gasped. "You're a pilot. That sounds really exciting."

"I love it. I've loved it for as long as I can remember. Never wanted to be anything but a pilot. It's kind of weird. My parents died in a plane crash, so you'd think I'd want to run as far away from a plane as I could. My daddy was the one flying that plane, and I always feel closer to him when I'm up there in the air."

"I think that's wonderful that you share that love of flying with him." She could only imagine the feeling he got from his flying.

"Let me take you for a ride."

Her heart jolted at that. "Seriously? That is an offer I'll take you up on." She was so excited after having had such a bad day that she threw her arms around his neck and hugged him. His arms went around her and for a moment he pulled her close, like the night they'd danced.

He smelled so good and she wanted to lay her head on his shoulder, but she came to her senses, realizing she'd thrown herself at him. "I'm sorry." She pulled away. "I've never been in a plane before, so this is really exciting to me."

His smile warmed her heart.

"I remember how giddy I was the first time I got to go up in a plane, so I completely understand."

They smiled at each other. And her heart kind of tripped over itself. Beck was kind and generous and unlike any man she had ever met. But she needed to remember he was out of her league.

"Take my number and I'll call when I get back into town. And if you decide to take me up on my other offer, it's still out there."

They exchanged numbers then he winked at her. "Remember the offer stands."

She sighed as she watched him get in his truck and then drive away. There was a lightness in her step as she went inside and closed the door.

She was going flying with Beck.

And there was absolutely no more crying on his shoulders.

No more.

CHAPTER SIX

The sun was going down as Beck landed his plane on the airstrip behind his cousin Todd's winery on Thursday evening. He had enjoyed his last two days flying and he had had a lot of time to think while he carried clients from New York to the West Coast, and then he had to pick up people from the West Coast and carry them to Houston. It worked out great. Today, he had had a short flight; he'd done it that way on purpose so that he'd be back here in time to have tomorrow off. His phone rang as he taxied to a stop. He had left his truck near the field so that he could drive to his house after he landed and not have to rely on one of his cousins or brothers to pick him up. He had had this deal with Granddaddy on his mind and on top of that, he had had Mollie's situation.

He had known she wouldn't take a loan from him. He had gone over in his head how to figure out a way to save her ranch. He had even toyed with the idea of just calling the bank and buying the ranch but that was ridiculous. She had her pride, and she would probably be furious with him for doing that. But he had decided that if it came down to it, he would do that. Unlike his granddaddy thought, he had his own money that had nothing to do with the charter. He wasn't destitute or desperate; the only thing that his granddaddy had over him was the charter business and his love for it. And the fact that he had built it.

He was still thinking as he walked toward his black double cab GMC and climbed in. *Was he really going to do this?* Driving out of the back area of the winery, he headed down the main winery's drive to the road. Todd waved at him from the field. Turning his truck, he drove down the lane, parked, and then walked to where Todd was tending to a vine of grapes. His cousin loved his winery. He loved the jelly making part the best. There was good reason nobody made jelly like McCoy Stonewall Jelly Farm and Winery.

"What're you doing? I saw you fly in. How's it going?" Todd grinned.

"I'm doing all right. I guess I must have lost my mind because I'm contemplating going through with this, just like y'all did."

"Yeah, it sounds terrible, but when it comes down to it, you get to thinking about it a little bit and it's almost hard not to do it. Although my situation was a little bit different than everybody else's because, well, Ginny, you know, was a friend of Allie's and she kind of needed the same thing I needed. So it was, like, I don't know…what's the word…destiny. It worked out well for me, so I'm just going to tell you to do it. It's kind of a win-win situation. Who do you have in mind?"

"I met her the other night. I went to the Gruene dance hall—just needed to get away before Granddaddy had his little talk with me. And I met her. And she's going through a really hard time. I've been trying not to think about it, but it's bugging me that I might be able to help her with this and, you know, help myself at the same time. But you know, she's a stranger…she would have to really, really be desperate to do this. I just called Wade, you know, because Allie was really desperate in a different way. And now that I think about it, I guess your Ginny—her desperation was more similar to Mollie because it had to do with land that has been in the family for forever. Like I told Wade, I just don't want to take advantage of her."

Todd set his pruning shears down in the basket, and took his cowboy hat off and slapped it on his thigh as he squinted at him. "All you can do is ask. Me and Ginny, we didn't even really like each other when we started out but because it was mutually beneficial, we did it. So, if there's any chance at all that you think you can help this woman, then offer it to her—let it stand and she can decide."

"Yeah, that's the same thing Wade said. I can't decide if it's because I don't want to take advantage of her or if I'm dragging my feet because I just don't want to do it."

"Beck, I've never taken you as a chicken. I've looked at you as an innovator. You saw what you wanted and you went for it. You built an amazing business—you don't want to see that go down the tubes."

Bitterness grabbed him by the throat. "No, I don't. I heard this week that Granddaddy's selling my business, take everything that I've worked for and sell it, most likely at a dirt cheap price, just to make me mad. That's his one big thing that he's got on me—he knows I don't want him to sell it. See, he knows if he still has the McCoy name on it, still has a semblance of the thing I've worked for, I could live with that. But if he sells it...shoot, it will have somebody else's name on it. It will dismantle my concept and it will be theirs. It will be as if everything I worked so hard for never happened. I can't stand that. My granddaddy is a piece of work."

Todd laughed. "Yes, he is that—as my granddad was, too. The way I look at it is we're cut from the same cloth. I'm not saying what they're doing is right but I do think we can answer the call. I like that I did it—put myself out there and Ginny did, too. Come on—do it. If nothing else comes of it, at least you have saved your legacy and helped whoever this girl is save hers."

"I'm probably bringing her out here tomorrow— going to take her up in the airplane, I think. Kind of spend the day getting to know her, then decide whether I'm going to ask her. If you see me, don't come blurting out anything. Because there's no guarantee that I'm going to go through with it at the end of the day. I'll have to swallow my pride to do what Granddaddy wants me to do. To bow down to his demands and marry to save my company."

"You can do this. We all did it and it was a blessing. Good luck. I won't say anything but good luck."

"Thanks. I'm going to need it."

* * *

Mollie's phone rang as she was finishing up feeding her goats for the day. She hadn't heard from Beck since the night he'd come to offer her a loan and saved her from the snake. Seeing his name on her phone sent her heart into a crazy somersault.

Get a grip.

"Hello." Her voice sounded breathless and she could do nothing to hide it. She hoped he thought she'd been running across the field or something, not breathless from talking to him.

"Mollie, sorry I haven't called all week but I'm in town and I've got tomorrow off. Are you still game for a ride in the sky? I can pick you up about ten, if that's good for you?"

Good for her? Oh, yes, indeed. "Sure, but you don't have to pick me up. That's a long way for you to drive. I can drive to wherever you have your plane."

"No, I'll come get you and then I'll bring you back home. Not a big deal. Are you still excited to go?"

"Yes. Very excited."

"Good. Plan for all day, if you've got the time."

All day? "I don't really have anything planned for tomorrow. You know, my normal...I'm going to feed all my goats in the morning and my livestock and chickens and probably run from a snake or something.

But I can do all that before you come at ten."

He laughed. "If you need me to check your chickens when I get there, I'll do that. And your water well, too. I don't want you running from a snake again."

"Thanks, but I can do it. I've been practicing my sprinting, so I'm good."

She hung up, still feeling disbelief that she was actually going to go for her first plane ride tomorrow and in a Learjet. Last night, she'd looked Beck up and McCoy Flight Charters, and he'd looked so handsome, standing on a runway in front of his fleet of planes. He'd surprised her because he wore his black cowboy hat and a T-shirt, looking so casual and sexy and he'd been grinning proudly. She saw another one of him in his business suit, too, but in most everything she saw of him, he was casually dressed. He was a casual guy and he looked really good that way. Again, she told herself to hold down the hormones and admiration or she was going to get hurt, but she couldn't help it. Obviously, this was her month for getting hurt and at the moment, she was feeling reckless.

She could hardly sleep that night. By ten o'clock the next morning, she had been pacing the front yard for a while before he drove up the lane. She had put on a pair of white jeans and a hot-pink shirt and a pair of sandals and wondered whether she had worn the right kind of clothes. She didn't know what they were going to do—whether they were going to land somewhere or make a circle and come right home. She felt dizzy with excitement as he got out of his truck.

He grinned as he walked toward her, that black hat pushed back at a cocky angle. He looked dangerous— dangerous to her heart—and she knew it without question.

"You want me to feed those chickens for you?"

She laughed, glad to have something else to focus on rather than her own fantasy. "No, I've taken care of it. But thanks for asking."

He laughed and his eyes twinkled. "Well, you look pretty today. I guess that sounded funny—you always look pretty. But, anyway, come on. It's going to be a good day. I've got our flight plan and a few surprises."

"Well, what are we going to do? I thought we

were just going for a little spin."

He opened his truck door and waited for her to climb in. She did, and oh, he smelled heavenly as she scooted into the seat.

With his hand on the top of the door, he looked at her with a boyish grin. "We are going for a little spin, but it doesn't mean it has to be a short little spin…it could be a long little spin. Anyway, all you have to do is tell me when you're ready to come home, and I'll bring you back. Until that time, I've got the day planned out. So long as you don't get up in the sky and decide you can't stand it, we're going to be fine."

Excitement bubbled up like champagne inside her. "Well, I can't turn that down. I don't even know why you have decided to take this interest in me but I'm going to take it while I can get it."

His eyes seemed as if they shadowed a little bit on that. Then he closed her door, went around the front, and climbed in. It took them about thirty minutes to get from her place to the McCoy winery. He drove through the main entrance and past the vineyards. It was a beautiful place. The plane was waiting for them, all alone on a long airstrip at the back of the vineyards.

It struck her then just how far their worlds were apart from each other. The man owned his own Learjets and the family had their own private airstrip.

She couldn't even contemplate how much money that involved. She felt kind of like Cinderella, she realized…all too aware that the clock would strike midnight soon enough.

She'd been looking for a rental all week that she could afford and hadn't found anything yet but she was hopeful. Having this plane ride had given her something to look forward to, but it was just spending time with Beck that lifted her spirits.

A few minutes later, they were on the plane. It was beautiful on the inside, with more room than it appeared from the outside. The rich, buttery leather seats were inviting and empty. It was just her and him on this trip, and she could barely believe it.

He motioned for her to come into the cockpit with him. "You'll sit here." He motioned to the seat beside his, then helped her buckle in before he took his seat.

Soon, with a smile and a wink, he revved the

engine and they took off down the runway.

It was the most exhilarating experience she'd ever had as the wheels lifted from the ground and then they were in the air. The land dropped away the higher they rose into the sky. She gasped and could not help the giddy smile that played across her face as she whirled toward him.

"I can't believe you get to do this all the time."

He laughed. "Yeah, me either. Now, just lean back and relax for the ride."

She stared out at the beautiful blue sky and it felt as if all the worries in her life had fallen away with the land as they reached the clouds. It was mesmerizing. Completely mesmerizing.

"Kind of makes you think a little bigger when you're up here?"

"Yes, I was thinking just that. It's uplifting, isn't it?"

"I've always thought so. My cousins and my brothers all have different interests. We were all raised together but all love different things. For me, it was the sky. I loved the sky before I even got up into it."

"I can see why."

They rode in silence for a while and she drank in the peace, watching the clouds around them.

"How's it going this week? Did the bank reconsider?"

"Reconsider? No. I've been busy packing the last two days. And it hurts. But I'm kind of forcing myself to come to grips with it. This is a very welcome diversion."

"Good. Glad to help. So, you're still not interested in trying to save the ranch?"

"I've tried to rack my brain to figure out a way, and I can't. Your offer of a loan was really sweet, but I still can't take you up on it. The ranch is doomed, and I know it. I'll live. It could be worse, you know. I'm just trying to be grateful."

He nodded, but she got the feeling he wasn't happy.

CHAPTER SEVEN

Beck's destination was Destin, Florida. It was a short flight. He decided he'd wished he'd planned a longer one but he had more than a plane ride planned.

They'd talked about her job and about all the people from Stonewall that she was meeting. The family's long-time friend Penny and some of her buddies had been coming in on a regular basis, and she had liked them a lot. She'd also met his sister-in-law Blaze and been startled when Blaze had told her that she had been a chauffeur.

"I can't even believe a woman would want to do that. But I think it's kind of cool. I would probably get somebody lost if I was trying to be a chauffeur."

He laughed. "Well, there's probably not been a time when a chauffeur didn't get somebody lost, so that wouldn't be the end of the world."

She grew quiet for a minute as she studied the land below them. Then she looked at him. "I guess. But, I mean, there's things I've just never thought about that are just so not traditional that people would do. I guess I'm starting to kind of think if I'm not going to be living on the ranch, what will I do?"

Take my offer, he wanted to say. "You'll figure something out. If you don't end up figuring out a way to keep it." He was still holding out hope that she would take his offer—or maybe his new offer, if he decided to make it.

"That's not going to happen. I'm thinking about other options. Not that I can be a chauffeur or a pilot of an airplane, but I figure I'll probably need to find something other than working at Dixie's. Although my tips have been pretty good. I'm really surprised at what I'm bringing in. I don't know—I just haven't given it a lot of thought. But we're not going to talk about me today. We're going to focus on this awesome trip."

He wanted to talk about her. He wanted to convince her to…what? *Marry him?*

The thought churned inside him like a building storm. And it was building in intensity when he landed the plane at a small airport near Destin.

He hadn't really known where to bring her, but he wanted to give her a good ride. He wanted to brighten her day, and nothing seemed to brighten people's day like a trip to the beach. Pretty blue water and a nice meal overlooking the bay was the perfect place to land for lunch.

She looked at him as they flew into the airport. "I can't believe that we're already in Florida." Her smile was huge.

He liked her smile.

"And that water is amazing, isn't it?"

Her eyes sparkled and he loved seeing the excitement in her. *This was what she looked like when she wasn't weighed down with worry.*

He stared at her. "It's amazing." He smiled. "One day we'll take a longer plane ride and I'll take you down to Key West. Talk about blue water—it's beautiful. Or we could fly to the Bahamas."

Her eyes got wide. "Really?"

"Hey, I like to fly, even on my days off."

He'd ordered an open-air Jeep to be waiting for them, and he enjoyed her delight as they buckled in and he drove them along the ocean road. Her excitement caused him to realize how he had been taking a lot of things in life for granted. He flew everywhere; it wasn't anything for him if he decided to go eat at his favorite restaurant—he flew there, like today. He'd just loaded up and here they were.

Traffic wasn't bad as they drove down the oceanfront drive, past up a lot of the major resorts and then took a cutoff that led to a small beachfront restaurant. It had a surfboard out front and a crazy-looking little cartoon character dude to welcome them. He walked around and helped her out of the Jeep. When he took her hand, he felt an electric shock as he touched her. He hadn't gotten used to the way that she sparked jolts of awareness through him just with a touch or even a twinkle in her eye.

And then there was that feeling of complete

empathy when she lapsed into worry. He could tell when she was doing it. Her brow would crease in the center just a little bit and then she would bite her lower lip. She had a lot on her shoulders, and it bothered him, made him really aware how little he truly had to worry about in his own life. He had always had a soft place to land if he had needed it. Until now. Until Granddaddy had flipped his hat on end, and made Beck question his sanity.

He pushed those thoughts out of his head for now. This was about lunch and keeping a lady smiling.

She smiled at him, and he smiled back. "This is a cute place. And you told me it had really good food, so I'm expecting that it probably does. It could have the worst food in the world, and I would still be happy after that amazing plane ride. This is just icing on the cake. To think, I've never ever eaten at a restaurant on the beach. I'm excited."

Clearly the woman needed to get out more. There was more to life than her farm. "You need your horizons opened up a little more. I brought you here because I love this place and wanted to ease your mind for a little while."

"You've succeeded."

They walked inside and his friend Lee Jordan waved at him from behind the bar as he spotted them. "Beck McCoy. Come on in. I saved you your favorite table for you and your lady. Just head on out there and I'll be there in a few minutes."

He didn't correct Lee on the "your lady" comment but saw the pink blush that came to Mollie's cheeks. "Thanks, Lee. I'll introduce you to my friend when you get out there."

"Sounds good."

They strode through the crowded interior and out onto the patio that stretched out over the water. He went straight to their table. "I love this table. It's right on the corner and you can see the water from behind or straight down. There are usually fish there. You never know what will swim up. I've seen a manatee once and tarpon, big shiny silver fish, and sometimes the porpoise show up."

"Wow. That sounds great but I'm just grateful for the water."

As they sat, a group of pelicans soared by, low over the water.

"Look! Oh, my goodness, look how they fly. Like they're on a mission."

"A food mission to scoop up fish." About that time, one did just that. "See there?"

She laughed. "That's really cool. Look at him gulp it down—oh my goodness, one big bite. I need to get a picture of that."

"Put your phone on the table so it's ready the next time he flies by."

She pulled it from her small purse and laid it on the table, then met his gaze. "This is all normal to you."

"I have to say, it is. Usually I'm flying somebody in for something—you know, like someone's wanting to fly down for vacation—and then instead of just turning around, I'd come here for lunch. Lee and I went to school together, and he opened this place and it's done well. He's got excellent food, so I like to come by and see him whenever I can."

"And you do this in other places too?"

"Yes. If I'm flying somewhere, I'm going to find out where the best food is and try it out. Sometimes my flight schedule is so busy that I have no time for side trips, but these days, since I have my crew, I can pick and choose my destinations. I guess I'm kind of spoiled...I just take what I want these days." He frowned, realizing that wouldn't be the case much longer. "Things are about to change, though."

They stared at each other. She swallowed and looked out at the water. "I might do better just to leave Stonewall," she said, absently. "Maybe I should move to a place like this and start over again, fresh. That water is beautiful. I can't imagine waking up to that pretty water every day. I'm not tied to the ranch any longer, so after I save a little money, I could move wherever I want to. Nothing ties me to Stonewall anymore, so, thinking optimistically, the world is at my fingertips. I can do anything I want and this..." She smiled into the breeze; it lifted tendrils of her hair and she closed her eyes, letting the sun beat down on her pretty face.

He watched her, his gut churning. She was

beautiful and heartbreaking in this moment, at this crossroads in her life, a place she didn't want to be but was struggling to make the most of it.

He questioned himself in that moment. *What if she was right? What if this was her time to find a new life?*

She looked back at him then. "This—it's wonderful. Can you imagine? I mean, I like Hill Country and everything. It's been my home—it's always called to me—but, you know, I could get used to coming to work at a restaurant here like this every day and waiting on people with that view."

"Yeah, I guess you could. You're right—you don't have anything holding you back. If that's what you wanted to do, you could do anything you wanted to."

She toyed with her napkin. "Maybe get a job at a place like this. I bet I would make really good tip money and then in the evening, maybe take some online business courses. Who knows, I might want to open a place like this myself." She smiled, big and engaging. It was almost as if her heart were in that smile, but it wasn't too happy. As though she forced it.

"You could fly in and come by and eat at my place. That sounds like a really cool thing. I may have to ask your friend for some advice on all that."

"Ask me what?" Lee asked, striding up.

Lee was an ex-football player at A&M, where they had gone to college together. He was big, tall, and good-looking, and he smiled a bright-white smile at Mollie. She looked up at him and she was probably interested. Lee had never had a problem with the ladies. He gave her his *you're-beautiful-let's-talk* smile. A knot of possession tightened in Beck's chest. He wanted to tell him to back off and not play games with Mollie. But he kept his mouth shut. He had no claim on her.

"I was just telling Beck that I might want to move to the coast. I don't have anything really holding me to Stonewall anymore and I'm rethinking my life. I wouldn't mind working somewhere on a beach. This is beautiful. I just don't see how you don't wake up every morning and pinch yourself at the beauty around you."

Lee threw his head back and laughed. He crossed his arms and grinned at her, a genuine grin this time.

"Well, I kind of do. I love Texas, myself. You know, I went to school at A&M with Beck, and I loved it. But now I have the best of both worlds—family in Texas and a home here. Now, don't get me wrong, my heart always belongs to Texas, but this is my second choice and I go home and visit my family often."

"That's nice. I'm sure your family always likes when you come home."

"Yeah, and they like to come visit me, too. They love it here—they have a beach house that they bought not too far from here. That way they have a place to stay whenever they come not too far from my place. I've got a little piece of heaven both here and in Texas. So you and Beck here aren't dating?"

He looked at Beck, and Beck could have kicked him because he knew he was fishing.

"No. Beck's just my friend. He found out I had never flown in an airplane and so he took me for a plane ride to eat lunch here."

She was about as innocent sounding as a newborn calf. And he could see that Lee was startled, too, by how open and innocent she was.

Lee was not an idiot. He grinned at Beck. "I see. Yeah, you always are a nice guy like that. Anyway, if you decide you need a job and you want to move down here, you just come see me."

"Thank you. But I honestly wasn't saying that to get you to offer me a job. Right now, I've got a lot of possibilities in my life and I'm just thinking about what I'm going to do."

Beck knew what he liked. He looked at Mollie. "I usually have his fish tacos. They're the best you can get, but you look at the menu and order whatever you want."

"I'll just have the fish tacos. If they're as good as you say they are, then I don't want to pass those up."

"Coming up."

She smiled again, brightening the deck with its beauty.

Lee walked away and then looked back over his shoulder. He was behind Mollie and she couldn't see him; he gave Beck a hitched brow. Lee would be giving Beck a phone call later tonight. Beck wasn't sure what he'd tell him. He wanted to tell him they were dating. Truth was, he was interested in Mollie and that only complicated everything even more. He was still undecided about whether he was going to ask her to marry him—a fake marriage, but it could turn into a real-life fiasco.

He had a feeling that Mollie would think that was the strangest thing ever to be offered and that she would turn him down flat.

CHAPTER EIGHT

Mollie was still in shock that she was actually in a whole other state with this amazing guy—this dream guy who, a few days ago, she hadn't even known existed and she had for some weird reason, so unlike herself, gone up to at a dance hall and asked him to dance and then spilled her guts to him. That's all she could think—she was just in such a weird spot that she had acted out of character and now she had flown with him in a Learjet to Destin, Florida and was eating lunch at a great restaurant that had amazing fish tacos. She didn't even think she liked fish tacos but goodness gracious, those were so good. And now they were walking on the beach. It was crazy. It was a little overwhelming.

She was not Cinderella but Alice in Wonderland and had fallen in the rabbit hole and was in an entirely different dimension as they walked along the beach after lunch.

She had taken off her shoes and carried the sandals between her fingers. As they strolled beside each other, her feet sloshed through the cool water. She hoped to see a sand dollar among all the seashells, and she picked up a few of them. They were beautiful. She clutched them in her free hand, planning to take them home so she'd have something to help her remember this day. It was delightful, having the cool water rolling in, with its soft waves licking at her feet. The soothing sound eased the tension that kept trying to settle between her shoulder blades when her thoughts drifted back to reality. She was soon—too soon—losing her ranch.

"Penny for your thoughts," Beck said beside her.

She glanced at him. To her surprise, he'd removed his boots and left them in the Jeep, along with his hat. His jeans were rolled at the ankle and his feet were bare; his dark hair ruffled in the breeze. The man could fit in anywhere.

"I keep getting lost between this fairy-tale day that you've brought me on and then real life keeps coming in, where I have to make such big decisions and everything."

"I'd hoped this might help ease some of your stress. And I was having a craving for fish tacos."

His smile touched a chord inside her. She stopped walking and faced him. "Why are you doing this for me? You are probably the strangest guy I have ever met. You barely know me and yet you're being so kind to me. I keep thinking there has to be another reason, or you just feel terribly sorry for me."

His expression tightened. "I did this because, well, you're nice, and I thought you would enjoy it."

Something about the intensity of his expression and then the kindness of his words didn't ring exactly true to her. "But there has to be a reason. I mean, I'm just a girl you met in a bar."

He stepped back. "Why do you keep putting yourself down like that?"

Anger swept through her then. Anger she'd been

holding inside ever since the reading of the will. Oh, she'd let the tears roll and the grief lay her out, but this anger had been lurking below the surface. "I guess because I feel that way right now. I stuck my head in the sand and let all the warning signs that something wasn't right pass right over my head. So, I can't help it—I feel really stupid right now for letting everything in my life get to this point. How could I have been so naive?"

In an instant, he had his hands wrapped around her arms, tugging her close. "Stop. You're not stupid. It's not your fault that your granddaddy didn't tell you or maybe lost his ability to make clear decisions. Your granddaddy probably, in his right mind, would have never done something like this to you, from what you say about him. So you were caught completely unaware and in circumstances that should have never happened. That doesn't make you stupid. Or needy. It makes you human. You needed a friend that night at the dance. You needed someone to talk to and I'm glad you came to me and not some other cowboy in the place. I've been concerned and just want to make sure you're all right."

She breathed in a deep breath, his words sinking in. It was true, all that he said, but she just couldn't get past the fact that she hadn't even thought to see whether her granddaddy was acting right in the decisions he was making about the ranch. So many things she should have been thinking about as she realized how forgetful he was getting. She had been in her own little world.

The salty wind took her breath away for a moment and she turned slightly. "I know what you're saying is true, but I should have seen it coming. Look!" She gasped as a wave came in and through the clear, sun-kissed wave, the black outline of two stingrays with white dots on their backs were visible. "Stingrays. They're beautiful."

"Let's follow them." Beck led her down the shoreline in pursuit as the stingrays swam in and out of the sand as they followed the shoreline. It was as if they, too, were strolling along the beach.

People all along the walk stopped to watch them but she and Beck were the only ones who followed them. After a while, the stingrays slowly disappeared back into the deep water, as if they'd been figments of her imagination.

"Wow, so beautiful. Thank you for bringing me here. I have had such a good time. But don't you have to get back?" She hoped he wouldn't return to their other conversation.

He checked his watch, a very expensive watch, she thought. It glistened against his tanned wrist. "You're probably right. I should have you back just in time for your little goats to eat."

"That would be a good thing. If I don't get back in time to feed them, they'll probably eat the barbed wire to get out and then eat a hole through my door and eat me out of house and home. You ever see how much a goat can eat or what it can eat? It's crazy. I mean, they can eat Sheetrock and even plywood. I've never seen anything like it."

He laughed. "I've never raised a goat before. They sound ominous."

"I wouldn't go that far. They're adorable. They can be trouble but they're also good pets, especially when they're little. I'm going to have plenty of them. I can give you one, if you want. Just can't tell the bank if I gave you one since they technically are about to belong to them. I don't know if they've counted my goats yet."

"I don't think a goat's what I'm looking for but thanks for the offer anyway."

They smiled at each other and then, as if thinking alike, they turned and started back up the beach to where they parked the Jeep.

Yup, it had been an amazing day and within minutes, they were back on the plane and flying back through the sky. She was about to come out of the rabbit hole; she was about to get back to real life.

Tomorrow, she would probably think this was just a dream. *Too bad.*

* * *

The sun was just starting to go down in a red and golden display of beauty as he parked his truck in front of her house. Her heart was about to thunder out of her chest as she looked at him and gave him what she hoped was not too sappy of a smile. She felt sappy after the day they'd had together.

"I've had such a good time today. Thank you. It was unbelievable and something I never dreamed I would do. But, anyway, it's back to real life...my goats are calling my name." She smiled wider and hoped it conveyed how much she had enjoyed herself.

"I had a good time, too. I'm going to check your chicken house and water well house for unwanted guests and then I'll help you feed your goats."

He was already out of the truck before she could stop him. She climbed out and closed the door. Her nerves were rattled. "You don't need to stay. You don't have to help me do that. Honestly, just because I got scared the other day, there's not usually snakes in there. I'm just jumpy."

He was already striding across the grass toward the chicken coop. She had to hurry to catch up to his long strides.

"Honestly, to think to see a snake so soon again— it's probably not going to happen." She needed him to go. She was a little too infatuated with the guy, and if he didn't go, she was probably going to make a fool of herself. She didn't want to appear any more needy than she already did. And she didn't want to give in to the desperate need to throw herself into his arms.

That would *not* show him she wasn't needy.

He opened the clasp on the door to the chicken coop, ducked his head, and went inside. "My grandma used to have a chicken coop and when I was little, I would go in and get the eggs for her. I had to kill a few chicken snakes back then too."

"Your grandma had a chicken coop?" His grandma had to have been wealthy also; the idea that she had a chicken coop was kind of strange to her.

"My grandma liked fresh eggs. And she loved giving fresh eggs to her friends. Or anyone who wanted them. And she could can and put up vegetables, and she would share those pickled okras and canned beans. I guess it's not canned—it's cannisters…is that what you call them?"

She chuckled. "Jars—she probably put them in glass jars with metal lids."

"Yeah, that's what she did. She also froze some stuff too. I remember she'd do corn and she'd put it in those bags after she made it into creamed corn. I haven't tasted anything that good since she died. We didn't have the gardens after Grandma died and I miss all that."

She really needed to let him go. "I've got some creamed corn in my freezer. My grandma loved to put up fresh vegetables also. She probably would have been about the same age as your grandma." She tried to fight herself on inviting him to dinner. They'd spent all day together; he didn't want to stay for dinner. But he really sounded like he'd like some fresh creamed corn. And as far as she was concerned, her grandmother's recipe beat everybody's. It had nothing to do with her. She did it exactly how her grandmother had taught her and it was a tradition that she carried with her all these years.

It hit her then that she'd be walking away from that garden they had had all those years and she'd never have creamed corn anymore. You could grow tomatoes and green peppers in pots, and squash and all kinds of things but it took some land to grow corn.

"You've got some more eggs." He held up two eggs. And grinned like a kid.

"Looks like I do. That's awesome. And no snake."

"Nope. He's probably over there in your water well."

"Don't remind me. Do you want to stay for supper? My grandma taught me how to put creamed corn up and I have some in the freezer. It wouldn't take but a little bit to cook it. And I could fry you up a pork chop—I had them sitting out in the refrigerator."

He came out of the chicken coop and locked the gate behind him. "I don't want to impose. You're probably ready to get rid of me."

Oh, she was not ready to get rid of him, but she needed him to go. She was so in trouble. But he had done such a kind thing for her today. "No, I'd like you to stay. I can pay you back with supper for all the things you did for me today. And then you can go home, and we can call it even."

"I promise I won't stay too late."

They stared at each other and she wanted to say he

could stay as long as he wanted, but she knew she needed to say, *please leave now*. Instead, she turned and headed toward the house. Only halfway across did she remember that she hadn't fed her goats. "Let me take the eggs and I'll put them in the chair. Then we'll feed the goats."

Their hands touched as she took the eggs, and jolts of electricity shot up her arms. "Thanks. Just wait right there. I'll be right back."

She hurried to the porch and set the eggs in a little basket that sat on the tabletop by her chair there. Then she turned and hurried back across to him, looking better than any guy ought to look. She was breathless when she arrived beside him. "Okay, come on. Let's go meet my kids. They're going to love you. They might even try to eat your shirt."

He laughed.

She looked over her shoulder at him and grinned. "I'm not kidding. They might eat your shirt."

CHAPTER NINE

He hadn't realized how many goats she had. He followed her into the pen and around the corner of the old barn that it wrapped around and was startled when he saw concrete culverts about four feet in diameter stacked on top of each other. There were about ten of them, and goats stood inside each of the culverts. And one stood on top.

There were goats all around and as they walked into the pen, a bunch of small goats ran to her, dancing around her ankles. They jumped sideways and flipped and sprung up and down and did all kinds of crazy stunts. While he was distracted by them and Mollie, an old goat with short horns charged straight at him and ran right into Beck's hip. It hit him so hard it bounced back two feet.

"Ow!" Beck yelped, looking at the goat that looked as though it was ready to go to war.

Mollie gasped. "I'm so sorry. Jasper, no!" She grabbed Jasper by the collar and pulled him back as the baby goats continued their antics around her feet. It was a regular circus. The goat looked at him as if it were ready to come back and get him.

"Looks like you have a guard goat or something."

"He thinks he is. I raised Jasper from a baby goat, just like these little fellas, and he's like the granddaddy of them all. He thinks he owns me. He's protecting me but sometimes he can get a little too rough. I don't normally bring people in here because of him, and I wasn't thinking. Are you okay?"

"I'm fine. I just won't turn my back on him. Okay, I can watch out for him now."

She let go of him and put her finger in Jasper's face. "You stay right there and don't ram my company again. I'll get your goat if you do."

He had a feeling the goat wasn't paying her any attention. But to his surprise, it stood right where it was and stared him down. He knew if he wasn't careful, the minute he turned his back on the goat, he might get butted in the rear.

She reached down and picked up a little bitty goat. It looked like it was the size of a kitten.

He couldn't imagine how little it must have been. "That looks like a cat, not a goat."

She laughed. "It's a dwarf baby, and yes, they're little. She'll grow up to be about the size of her mom—over there in the corner is its mom and daddy. She'll be littler than all of these around me, though. This is Tillie Mae. She's a cutie pie, isn't she?" She cuddled it against her cheek and the little goat rubbed its head against her cheek. Its little dark eyes studied him as it cuddled up with Mollie. Then Mollie held it out from her and made kissy faces at it.

He realized he wished that Mollie would make kissy faces at him. Which was something he didn't need to be thinking about.

He needed to be thinking about whether he was going to ask her to marry him—for business reasons.

His head was woozy with the thoughts that had

been whirling away on the plane ride back to Stonewall. He worried over the situation. He liked her, thought she was sweet and needed protecting, and needed help to save her ranch. But he'd seen the look in her eyes and knew she was attracted to him. He was to her too, but that didn't mean marriage and forever love and until death do us part. And he could not, would not mislead her.

It was time to get this done before any romantic thoughts got mixed up in the middle of all this. Because it would be strictly business.

She handed him the goat. "Here, you cuddle with this one while I get in here and I'll get them some feed. Watch your shirt, though." She smiled wickedly and he laughed.

The woman made him laugh more than he'd laughed normally.

He thought about that. He was serious but realized maybe too serious.

He followed her into the barn, and she scooped out the feed and then the animals just dove in. Then she took the baby goat from him and set it on the ground; it immediately ran to its parents. She let him out of the pen and then he followed her across the drive toward the house. Moments later, she had led him into the kitchen.

The house was old but comfortable. The kitchen was white, with white cabinets and counters. Red and white checkered curtains hung on the window above the sink and he noticed that the appliances looked really aged. The house probably hadn't been updated in a long time. Her appliances were a dusky gold color and the cracked linoleum shone with wax.

She opened the refrigerator and pulled out a pitcher of tea and a glass container with pork chops marinating in something. She set the tea on the counter, and then she opened the freezer and pulled out a plastic Ziploc bag with a yellow concoction inside.

She smiled at him as she dangled it from her fingertips. "Creamed corn like I promised. May not taste exactly like your grandmother's but I'm telling you, it's good. Not bragging on myself—believe me, it's my grandmother's recipe and I've done everything exactly like she did, so she'll get all the glory if you like it."

"I'm sure I'll love it. Just something kind of similar to my grandma's is a treat."

She motioned for him to sit down. "Have a seat. It won't take long for me to do this. I'll make you a glass of tea."

"Let me help."

"No. Remember, this is my treat...my way of paying you back for today."

He watched her work and sipped on his tea. He liked watching the way she moved. They spent the next thirty minutes talking about what they had done that day. He asked her questions about her goats, her garden, and found out that her gardening experience had come from her grandmother.

"Are you going to hate to give this place up when you've got so many roots in it? Sounds like your grandmother worked in that garden a long time."

She paused taking the pork chops out of the skillet and placing them on a plate. "I am. I'm going to miss it so bad, but I can't always look back. It's time to move on. Time to be brave. I think there's a whole new world waiting out there for me."

He could tell she was just putting on a show, that it was really a struggle for her. But he didn't know what else to say at that moment.

Ask her to marry you.

He ignored the voice in his head. Now was not the time. By the time they finished eating, he had to admit her grandma knew how to make creamed corn, because it was excellent.

"I might have to start growing me a garden at my house. You'll have to come show me how to make this stuff. It's amazing. And very similar to my grandmother's. I wonder if that's just a recipe that they all had back then."

"I'm sure that they all had similar ways. It's probably the seasoning that's a little bit different."

"Well, it was delicious and thank you. I guess I'd better go."

She stood and took his plate over to the sink. She'd cleaned as she'd worked and there wasn't much to do. She turned the water on, rinsed it off, and then set it in the other sink.

It hit him then that he wanted to go over to her and take her into his arms. And he wanted to kiss her.

He stood his ground. That was some dangerous territory he was trying to wander off into and he needed to be strong. He did not need to complicate things. She was vulnerable.

She turned from the sink and met his gaze, her eyes big. The room suddenly felt warm.

He stepped back a step toward the door. His heart did somersaults about the same way as the baby goats had been acting earlier. This was not good. His back bumped into the back door and she was still staring at him. The clock was ticking, and it was as if somebody punched a panic button. He could hear the alarms going off, he ignored them.

She took a step toward him. "Beck."

He had not opened the door. He had not walked out the door and closed that door between them. Nope, he still stood there with his back up against the door, holding it shut.

She took another step toward him and it took all of his willpower not to reach for her.

Another step toward him and then three. He could see trepidation and longing mixed in her eyes. And then she stood right there in front of him.

"Beck." Her word was breathless.

Her eyes never left his; despite knowing that this was not what he needed to do, he opened his arms and she walked right into them. Immediately, he lowered his mouth to hers and kissed her softly. She responded and he was lost.

And in big trouble.

* * *

What was she doing?

That was what the sane part of her brain was asking her as she gave in to the kiss that she had had no willpower to stop herself from wanting. She had just practically thrown herself at the guy but as he kissed her, the wretched feeling of aloneness that had been her constant companion since losing her grandfather eased. And as his warm lips moved over hers, she wrapped her arms around him and clung to him. Her hands tangled in his short, thick hair, tugging his head closer. She never wanted the kiss to end.

When he pulled back, she clung to him. Her heart pounded relentlessly and as she gazed into his dazed eyes, she realized that she had probably done something she couldn't take back.

"I'm sorry, Mollie. I shouldn't have done that." He put his big hands on her arms and set her away from him. "I should have left when I said I was going to."

Her cheeks burned. She was embarrassed by her actions. Ever since she had met Beck, she had acted out of character. "It's okay. It was just a kiss," she said flippantly. It was not just a kiss to her, but maybe he didn't need to know that. It might have been just a kiss to him.

"I'd better be going." He turned, opened the door, and then strode out onto the porch.

She was confused and wanted to run after him but stopped in the doorway, placing her hand on the doorjamb to give herself some balance. Trying not to say something stupid, she said nothing.

He didn't stop until he got off the porch and then he turned, yanked his hat off and held it in his hands. "I had a good time today. I didn't mean to kiss you like that. I'm sorry. Didn't mean to show bad manners."

She managed to find words. "I didn't think it was bad manners. I kind of threw myself at you." Well, *that* was embarrassing.

"Well, it's been a long day. I'll see you later." And with that, he got in his truck and drove away.

Her stomach felt bottomless, like she might go throw up, actually. She had thrown herself at Beck. And then watched him run like the dickens to get away from her. Yeah, he probably thought she was pathetic. *How was she ever going to live this down?*

* * *

Beck had royally messed up.

He walked into his house, went straight to the shower, climbed in and let the hot water wash over his body as he tried to get the look of complete despair on

Mollie's face off his mind. He had made her think he was completely rejecting her. He slammed his palm against the tiled wall and rested his forehead against the stone.

He could have kept kissing her forever. He had never expected or reacted to a woman like that before. He wasn't even sure what had happened. It scared him, actually.

CHAPTER TEN

Three days later, Mollie carried a plate of pancakes from the kitchen into the diner, past the table that Dixie called "Beck's table." Every time she passed that table, she thought about the man she'd thrown herself at and who'd kissed her and made stars fly in her head. The man who'd walked away and whom she hadn't heard from since.

She told herself that night after he walked out that she had really messed up, but she kept thinking that her phone would ring, and she could apologize for throwing herself at him. He'd probably only kissed her out of pity...but it hadn't felt like pity. Whatever it was, it had gotten out of hand. Now he probably couldn't even come to the diner and eat Dixie's breakfast that he loved so much because he'd see her.

It was a pitiful state that she had gotten things in.

She had been packing the last few days, keeping busy. She had so many of her boxes filled and ready for the U-Haul she'd rented to carry them to her new place. The affordable place she hadn't found yet. As she'd packed, her thoughts weren't on leaving the home she'd always known but on Beck McCoy.

Dixie had noticed something was wrong with her. She had already asked her several times over the last couple of days what was wrong. But Mollie kept telling her nothing was wrong, that everything was fine. Maybe if she kept saying that enough, she would believe it was true.

This was so crazy. She barely knew Beck McCoy. She had just gotten a girlish infatuation with the guy. He was, after all, too good to be true.

By the time she got off that afternoon, she had pretty much talked herself into a near nervous breakdown. She was so obsessed with the fact that she had kissed Beck McCoy and she needed to apologize.

Maybe she just needed to see him again, but she

wasn't going to own up to that need.

After getting into her old truck, she knew she was going to go out to his house and see whether he was home. She didn't even know where he lived. Somewhere on the McCoy Ranch, which was near the winery. She drove in that direction. She drove the winding road and went around a particularly wide curve. She saw the iron gates of the McCoy Stonewall Jelly Farm and Winery. And as she passed it, admiring the vines as she went, she went around another curve and across the street she spotted the sign for the McCoy Ranch. She saw the gate up ahead but knew she was too nervous to turn onto the lane and follow it to the big house. Besides, she knew he didn't live at the main house. So how was she going to find out where he lived?

She passed the entrance, driving slowly, curious about where Beck had grown up. She felt like a snoop. It was beautiful. She had never driven out this way to see the vineyards just rolling along the road. The pastures were well kept, perfect, so unlike her pastures that needed care. She pulled to the side of the road. Her mind went to the winery. It kind of gave her inspiration. She couldn't have a winery on her place, could she? Both her strawberries and her farm animals were about to be gone, and she had no way to save it. If only she'd figured out how to make a living from her land. She had little time to figure this out now. It was too late.

She sat there, biting her lip and thinking, when, to her surprise, Beck drove by.

Her heart immediately thundered in her chest. She realized when his brake lights went on and he pulled to the side of the road a little farther up that he had seen her, too.

He turned the truck around and came back and pulled to the side of the road in front of her. He immediately got out of the truck and walked to her window. "Mollie, are you having car trouble?"

"I'm good. Um, actually…" Her palms were sweating. *What was she doing?* "I actually came looking for you. I need to talk to you."

He studied her, looking as if he were trying to figure out the problems of the world. "I want to talk to you, too. But let's not do it right here on the side of the road. Follow me to my house."

He turned and sauntered back to his truck. She waited as he turned the truck around again and then she followed him several miles down the road. He then turned onto a paved entrance and they went through an automatic gate. After a few minutes driving along the paved drive, a beautiful stone and glass home appeared. Her toes curled as she was reminded again that Beck was definitely, completely out of her league.

What had she been thinking?

She should go. Now. Her heart had taken on an erratic rhythm, just like her life had since her grandfather died and she'd learned nothing was as she'd believed.

This house was something that would come out of an *Architect's Digest*—or at least, she thought that was the name of the right magazine. She was a *Country Home* or DIY magazine kind of woman and he…was this.

It was beautiful, a modern and country mixture with a lot of glass and stone. There were two huge chimneys and she wondered at the size of the fireplaces they were attached to. She was wondering that, sitting in her old truck, frozen to the spot, when he opened the door for her.

"Come inside."

"Maybe I should just go." She wanted to say never mind, she would go on home.

"No. Come inside."

Beck met her as she got out of her truck. She tried to look upbeat and not mortified even though she actually was very mortified. "I love your house. It's just beautiful."

He turned and glanced at it. "Thanks. I helped design it and had it built about three years ago. Come in. We can talk."

She followed him.

They stepped inside. They were in a hallway that looked like a connection between the garage and the house.

He closed the door after them. "It's down this way, the kitchen and the living area." The room had windows on the opposite wall from where they had come in, and you could see a lake and then the river. It was a beautiful view. The whole house probably had that view. She walked with him down the hall and into a large area that was a kitchen and living space combined. A gigantic fireplace rose up several stories. It was majestic.

Definitely out of her league. She turned to him.

He stood in the kitchen area. "Would you like a drink? I've got coffee, tea, and there's some wine in there…you know, we do have a winery. There's sparkling water…sodas…fruit juice?"

Was he nervous? Probably afraid that she was going to jump him again. She needed to get out of there. "Maybe some water."

"Water it is." He opened the refrigerator and pulled out two bottles of water. He twisted the cap on one and set it in front of her, then he twisted the cap on the other and quickly downed half the bottle. He sat on one of the barstools that were drawn up to the huge bar. There were like six of them.

She took a quick drink of her water and then sat down on a barstool, one down from him. She didn't want to crowd him.

"So you just live here part-time? It's really big."

"Lately, I've been coming here more often." He cleared his throat and put both hands around the water bottle. Both arms rested on the counter as he stared at the bottle. Something was on his mind.

She needed to get this done and leave. "Beck, I need to apologize for throwing myself at you the other night."

His head came up sharply and he met her gaze. "Yeah, about that. I don't want to give you the wrong idea. I took you on that flight to take your mind off your troubles."

How many times had he told her that? Her heart hadn't been listening. "I know—believe me, I know. For some crazy reason, I acted out of character. I went with the moment. And I regret it. I really regret it— that won't ever happen again. I just wanted you to know that. So you don't have to be scared of me or anything. You can come to the diner and have your breakfast, and I'm not going to throw myself at you or make you uncomfortable. As far as I'm concerned, it never happened. I just want to forget about it." Her skin heated and his gaze held hers with an expression she couldn't read. *Gee, she wished she could read minds.*

His eyes shadowed and he looked down at that water bottle again. She wanted to start talking again but she made herself remain quiet.

"You don't have anything to apologize for. I should have left. I was standing at that door and I let my head get a bit off base. I should have turned and walked out that door before you ever had a chance to do that. I'm sorry. I might have been putting off the wrong signals and I apologize if that's the case."

They stared at each other. She didn't really know what to say. She had gotten vibes from him but she just told herself that she was imagining it. But him saying that now…had he actually been wanting that kiss too? Just the idea was very confusing.

"Mollie, I need to ask you something. It's something I've been struggling with ever since that first night we met. I was actually at that dance hall that night just to think and then you showed up and I wasn't expecting you and, anyway, I have a proposition. I have a situation with my grandfather that is out of hand. I can't decide whether it's something I really want to do but I'm just going to lay it out here and let you decide. My family tells me I need to ask you and give you the chance to say yes or no instead of me assuming that you'll say no."

Now she was confused. "What?"

He took a drink of water. The bottle was almost empty. "My granddaddy has already forced all of my brothers and my sister to get married or lose their inheritance. They've all managed to take him up on his challenge, and it turns out they've all been able to marry happily. I've been very rebellious about this, and I don't appreciate my granddaddy telling any of my siblings that they have to get married or they lose out on things that they care about—not just inheritance but things that they've built from their own hands. It's down to me now and if I don't get married, then I lose my charter business. And I was prepared to do that. But I've learned he's planning on selling it at rock-bottom prices. That's what gets my goat and that's what's making me even consider this."

She stared at him, totally lost. "He's forcing you to get married?"

"No, I have to choose to let him force me to marry. So, to get straight to the point, Mollie, I need a wife and I was wondering if we could help each other out. It would be mutually beneficial to both of us. I need a wife for three months and after the three months, we'll get divorced and both walk away with what we want. You'll be walking away with your ranch free and clear, and some cash in your pocket too. You could start over, do whatever you wanted to. As a matter of fact, as part of the deal, I'll help you get the ranch fixed up and functional and profitable before the end of the contract. You would have a property you could make a living from and not worry about anything. What do you say?"

She had lost her voice halfway through his speech. *What?* She just stared at him. She wasn't even sure she actually understood what he was even saying. *Had she imagined what he had just said?* Maybe she was hallucinating? Surely, he wasn't suggesting that he *buy* her for three months. The very idea was insulting and unheard of.

She stood. "This whole time that you've befriended me, it was because you needed this from me?" The words had come out of her mouth before she even thought them, but it was the truth. It hurt. It actually stung really bad that all this time she had thought that he had maybe been coming around because he liked her. But it had all been for this. He needed something from her.

He stood. "No. Yes, I wanted something from you, but also I wanted to help you. And at first I wasn't even going to ask you. I only wanted to help you. That's why I offered to just give you a loan with no interest—because I knew you wouldn't take money from me, free and clear. Even though I could give it to you in the blink of an eye."

"Oh, that's not good. I don't want charity. I don't want to marry out of a need to save my ranch. I can't even fathom this." She was walking toward the door before she even realized it. Anger bubbled inside her.

"I have to go." She backed toward the hall. Beck

stepped toward her, a look of alarm on his face. "You don't need to come with me. I'm fine. I can see myself to my car."

She turned and hurried down the hall. She could not get out of there fast enough.

* * *

Beck hadn't expected her to react like this—maybe to tell him no, but not to run, not to have looked so stricken. He started after her. "Wait, Mollie. Come on, don't go." But she was already out the door. He followed her outside. "Mollie, I didn't mean to insult you."

She paused at her old truck, her hand on the door as he reached her. She turned toward him. "You might not have meant to but you did. I thought you wanted to be my friend. I've got to go." She slipped into her truck.

He didn't say anything; he just stood there, watching her go.

He hadn't expected her to take it so personal.

'Course, then again, had he really expected anybody to take this deal? He hadn't even wanted to offer this deal, so why was he surprised at her reaction? Because he had thought she and he got along, and she would think that it was a good deal.

Yeah, he had been wrong about that. And she thought he had just been using her. Turning, he went back into the house and stared at it as he walked into the living room. The house that soon wouldn't be his because once Granddaddy took his charter business, Beck was leaving. He raked his hand through his hair. This was just too messed up. But it was Mollie he worried about. She was hurting right now and all because he'd said everything wrong. Done everything wrong.

* * *

Mollie sat on her porch as she waited on the moving truck to arrive. She had been fed up after Beck's offer to buy her to save her ranch, and she'd called the bank and told them to just come get the ranch; she was leaving in two days. She had found a garage apartment which was in pretty bad shape, but it was over this little old lady's garage and the lady was willing to let her rent it. She had just happened to see it one day, driving to work, and it had caught her eye. It was cheap and the lady who owned it agreed to let her move in. Mollie just needed a place to go to. She needed to come to grips with the fact that this was no longer her home, these goats were no longer hers. She just needed to break ties with everything. It was going to break her heart no matter what. She rubbed the baby goat's head as she cuddled it in her arms. She had already been rocking it for a while, telling it good-bye. *Pretty pathetic when the only thing you had in life to tell good-bye was a goat.* Most people at least had a dog. She had a goat.

She was startled when she heard a truck coming and looked up to see Beck's truck fling toward her—not the U-Haul. Dust churned behind him. She braced herself to see him.

He climbed out of his truck, looking around at the boxes, his eyes blazing.

"What are you doing here?" she asked, not happy with her traitorous piece of junk heart that beat faster at the sight of him. That was just ridiculous.

He yanked his hat off and, holding it in his hands in a very contrite, apologetic way, approached her. "I came to apologize. I've had you on my mind for the last two days. I wanted to do this, but I needed to give you time to cool off. And then I was at the diner a few minutes ago, and Dixie told me you had hired a guy and moving van to come load your things up. That you already called the bank and told them to come take your ranch. She was upset. I am too. You don't have to do this."

She stood and set the baby goat on the ground. It immediately started jumping up and down and dancing around. "I don't have another choice. And besides, I'd rather leave on my terms. I'd rather leave a few days early rather than just stay here and prolong it."

"Don't do this. You don't have to marry me, but you also don't have to lose this place. For goodness' sake, take my offer of a loan. Low interest—it's a business deal, plain and simple...just a business deal.

The marriage suggestion would benefit both of us but I don't care at this point—this is about you."

He walked up and from his back pocket, he pulled some papers. He set them on the table beside where she stood. When she ignored them, he tried to hand them to her. "Don't be stubborn. Look at the papers. I had my lawyer draw them up for you. They're legit. I even put a one percent interest rate on it just to make you happy. I've also made it for a lot of years, but we can make it however long or short you want it. It's an investment for me. Believe me, I'm about to lose my business—I need an investment. Take the deal. Be a businesswoman and make something of this place. I won't have to feel guilty about you thinking I tried to take advantage of you. I never meant to take advantage of you. I only wanted to help you. So that's what I'm doing right here." He finally stopped talking and stared at her with eyes begging her to do what he was asking her to do.

She glared at him, her heart thundering. She needed to ignore that; instead, she needed to use her brain. Only her brain had gone fuzzy. He was offering her a business deal. A bank wouldn't give her a loan. He was giving her a business deal; she repeated the thought. She looked at him; he hitched a brow and looked contrite. She hated that look on him.

"I believe in you, Mollie. What you've got here— you can make something of it, if you'll just take the deal. There's no pity in it. There's no anything—it's strictly business. You can take it to your bank and ask them—they wouldn't give you a loan, but I'll give you a loan because not out of pity—again, I repeat that. And not out of wanting anything except a good investment. I'm a venture capitalist, too. I look for things that work and this could work. You can do this."

Her throat suddenly ached and tears threatened. Her pride stung that he had been around her and she had mistaken that as interest. But if she ignored that and looked at it strictly as business, he was making her an unbelievable offer. Guilt hit her that he was going to lose his charter business and yet he was still offering her this. Pulling her gaze away from his, she reached to pick up the papers. She thumbed through them, just as an act of something to do. She knew it was fair. She knew or believed that he wouldn't do anything underhanded and yet if she was going to call herself a businesswoman, she needed to read at least some of the contract. But her eyes blurred, and she couldn't read any of it. She blinked hard and willed her throat to work.

"Okay, I can do this. If you're sure?" It was a question.

"I've never been surer about anything, Mollie. You're a good person. You're good for this and you're going to make a return on this investment. You just never had the opportunity nor saw the reason to be involved out here and make your dream a living, breathing thing while your grandpa was alive. But there's so much you can do here. I see all kinds of possibilities. With that comes cash, too, to help you get a start. I guess I'd better say that in case you didn't read that there."

She looked at the sum. "How did you know how much?"

"I called the bank. The place is in foreclosure—it's no secret. I got the numbers and I worked it up. It's all legit."

She sank down into her chair. She bit her lip as she fingered the contract. She wiped the back of her hand across her damp forehead. A pounding of a headache was coming on. "All week, I've been wondering—well, the last few days since you talked to me at your house—why would your granddaddy try to force you to marry? Why would he take something you've worked so hard for? If he loved you, why is he doing that? It just doesn't make sense to me."

He leaned against the porch railing and crossed his arms. His hat dangled from his fingertips. "It started with my great uncle J.D. Uncle J.D., he was a pistol, you know. You never knew what he was going to do or what he was going to come up with. And he was very domineering as far as he liked getting what he wanted, and it worked really well for him in this life. He was an amazing businessman, but he was a good man, too. He had a great heart. He had lost his only son and daughter-in-law in an airplane crash—the same one that I lost my mom and dad in. My granddaddy is his brother, so the both of them lost their only sons. And the both of them took on their grandkids instantly—they didn't even hesitate." He stared out toward the pastures and her heart hurt for him.

"I'm sorry."

He nodded, his eyes drilling into her. "Thanks. Anyway, they both took their sons' kids into their homes, and with their wives, our grandmothers, they raised us. We had really good lives and we all grew up with a business sense and a drive for making our dreams come true. There's seven of us and, sadly, when Uncle J.D. died suddenly last year of a heart attack, the one thing he had always wanted, and he had never gotten was great-grandkids. He wanted them bad, but his three grandsons—my cousins—none of them were even thinking about getting married, not even close. Uncle J.D. had been telling them that he wanted great-grandkids. He usually got the last word and in this he did, too. He left it in his will that they had three months to marry and had to stay married three months. It started with my cousin Wade.

"My granddaddy saw what was happening and he decided he wanted great-grandkids before he died. And now it's my turn. I thought I could just walk away and not feel anything. But then I found out he's got plans to sell it and he knew that would get me, 'cause the people who work for me are my friends. It's just going to be sold off to the lowest bidder. My name will be taken off the business I worked so hard for... Granddaddy knew that's what would push me to try at least to go through with this."

Her heart was going crazy again. This was so unbelievable. "Wow."

"So, my cousin Todd, we had a talk, and he told me maybe with this deal, I could help somebody—not to look at it like some terrible thing. Though it was inconvenient that maybe I could bless somebody with this temporary marriage. Then I thought of you."

Guilt hit her in that moment. The truth of what he had said hit her. *He had thought he could be a blessing to her.* And she had jumped immediately to looking at it that he was trying to use her.

"Is that the honest truth? You were thinking about being a blessing to me and not using me?"

"That's the truth. I just want to be a blessing to

you and make your loan—it's low interest but it's still a good deal for me. Every little amount's going to help me rebuild my new charter business. You can be a blessing to me by taking this deal and giving me that interest."

* * *

Beck knew he had not made everything clear the day that she had first left his house and it had bothered him. Now, looking at her, he just wanted her to take the deal. He had had to use money of his own to secure the loan because he couldn't use anything that was involved with his charter business—his granddaddy's business, he amended. He was thankful that he had made other investments on the side and could offer this loan to Mollie. It left him in a little more vulnerable position with cash flow for his own recovery after he lost his charter business. But the more he had thought about it, the more he just couldn't *not* do this. It might take him longer than he had wanted, but the one thing he knew he could not feel good about was her thinking that he had been trying to use her. And only wanting her friendship because he had wanted her to marry him and keep him out of trouble.

"Go on, sign it. Let's get this over with." He heard a engine behind him and he looked over his shoulder at the mid-sized U-Haul coming up the drive. "Sign it and tell the guy in the truck to go home."

She bit her lip and looked from the truck to him. "Tell me about this deal with your granddaddy. What would I have to do?"

He shifted from boot to boot, her words unsettling. "Nothing. Other than marry me, there's no other clauses in it. Stay married for three months. We don't even have to share the same bedroom—which we wouldn't. Since it's a strictly business deal. Granddaddy's got some crazy notion that I wouldn't do the deal unless it was somebody who I can fall in love with and that the three months gives us the time to fall in love and stay together. That's it—that's his whole objective. But I promise you this is just business. You don't even have to think about all that. He's wrong. We will walk away. And you'll have cash and a ranch that's up and running. I get to go fly planes a few times a week, keep my business going, and then the rest of the time, I get to work here with you. We'll get this place in shape. But I've made peace with what I'm going to lose."

The driver of the U-Haul climbed out. "You folks order a U-Haul?"

Beck didn't say anything; he just looked at Mollie.

She looked at the man and then the contract. She moistened her lips with her tongue, looking very nervous. "Strictly business?"

"Absolutely. I give you my word."

She walked to the edge of the steps and then smiled at the guy. "I know I got you out here for nothing and I'm willing to pay for your time. But I don't need the U-Haul after all."

"You sure?"

She looked back at Beck.

He didn't say anything, just gave her time to make her own mind up. He felt a combination of trepidation and excitement at the same time.

She nodded. "I'm sure. I can write you a check

right now or you can send me a bill, whatever works for you."

"No, ma'am. We're just taking it back to town if you don't need it."

He got back in his truck and Beck watched as he backed out and drove back down the lane. Only after he had turned onto the road did she look at Beck.

"Sign it." He smiled.

She shook her head. "Not that one. We need a preacher and the other contract."

"You're marrying me?"

"Yes. It's the only right thing to do…partner."

CHAPTER ELEVEN

"**I** now pronounce you Mr. and Mrs. Beck McCoy."

Beck felt for Mollie. He held her hands as the justice of the peace said the words, and they trembled terribly bad. He squeezed them gently, feeling a powerful sense of protection over Mollie. He was grateful to her for what she had agreed to do. And he liked her very much, so that made this whole ordeal worth having to go through. And he planned with all of his heart to make sure that when he left, her place would be sustainable and profitable. And would be something she would always have and be proud of. He smiled at her, hoping to encourage her to stop trembling.

"You may now kiss your bride."

The justice of the peace's words startled him. *Of course, he was supposed to kiss her.* They hadn't even kissed since her kissing him that night. And he would be lying if he said he hadn't thought about that kiss several times. It had been a great kiss. He just didn't wish to think about it—didn't want to put too much emphasis on it because him and her thinking about anything romantic that had to do with this wedding was dangerous. For himself, he would always worry that if he hadn't done this, she might have fallen for someone else.

He knocked all the thoughts out of his brain. He was overthinking it. She looked at the justice of the peace and then back at him and he could see in her eyes that she was questioning whether he was actually going to kiss her or not. He waited too long. To make up for it, he stepped closer, put his arms around her, and pulled her against him as he lowered his lips to hers.

It was only going to be a brief kiss. But as their lips met, hers were so hesitant and he could only imagine that she was so worried about the fact that he didn't want to kiss her that he couldn't help himself— he kissed her. He kissed her with mind-boggling heat. It came from out of nowhere. The instant her lips touched his, he almost couldn't help himself. After a second, feeling a bit dazed, he pulled back.

The justice of the peace grinned. "Now, that looks like it's going to be a nice, healthy marriage. You two kiddos have a great day." His secretary smiled from where she stood as a witness.

Mollie still hadn't said anything. Holding her hand, Beck thanked them and led Mollie out of the office, down the hallway and out into the sunshine.

Once they were outside, he turned to her. "Breathe, Mollie. Breathe. We're going to be okay."

She looked so dizzy, he wrapped an arm around her and cupped her elbow on the other side of her body and just held her for a minute up against his side. "Are you all right?"

"I feel like such a wimp. You'd think I'd be prepared for this. But I guess I'm not." She inhaled again and then patted his chest. "I'm okay now, thanks.

Just kind of weird knowing that I'm married. Mrs. Beck McCoy."

He chuckled. "For whatever that means, but yeah, for now."

"Yes, for now."

Was there a shadow in her eyes when she said that?

"I guess, if it's okay with you, we'll head back to the house. I'm not in the actual mood to run into anybody. And we can just run by and grab a meal. How's that sound—take it home with us?"

"That sounds good. Whatever you want."

He hoped to the dickens that he was doing this right. But he figured the more emphasis they put on it being a real marriage wouldn't be a good thing, so they needed to keep it light and they needed to keep it on the business. That wouldn't be good for Mollie. He certainly didn't want to give her the wrong idea. Even though taking her to lunch or taking her out to celebrate seemed like the right thing to do, it also seemed like the totally wrong thing to do.

They were here and might as well get to work. He

hadn't told anybody they were getting married. He didn't want anybody here; he didn't want anybody wishing him well. When they got back to the ranch, he'd call his granddaddy's lawyer Cal and let him know they were married, that it was official and that the clock was ticking. He didn't plan to call Granddaddy.

He helped Mollie into his truck, which he had parked there in front of the courthouse. She smelled good today. She smelled of vanilla and some other floral scent mixed together. She smelled good enough to eat. Kind of reminded him of when his grandma would bake. He lingered in the doorway, letting that scent waft over him.

She looked up at him after she clicked the seat belt in.

"Mollie, I just want to tell you thank you. I want to say again, I think this is going to work out. I think it will be good for both of us. And I promise you, you're going to have a business that will sustain you and you'll be proud of it by the time we get through."

She nodded. "I'm glad to do it and I thank you

because I couldn't have done it without you. We'll make a good team."

"Yeah, a good team. Exactly."

* * *

"So, you're going to make a sustainable farm, but just look at all this acreage you have. Have you thought about peaches? I mean, this area, Stonewall—the peaches are amazing and there's a big call for them. You can grow a great orchard here. We need to look into that if you think that's something you want to do. I mean, that right there could be a great business."

Why, she had never thought about peaches. This area was known for their peaches; its peaches, its wineries, its grapes were amazing. Hill Country was just loaded with opportunity. Even prickly pear cactus could make jelly, and this was the perfect environment for it.

"I think the idea of peaches would be great. I wonder how much acreage it would take. And what about the irrigating and all of that?"

Beck stood with his arms crossed and studied the land. They had driven across the land early today, just looking at it. "You have more than enough room for an orchard and still have room for the calving business too. When we go into this, we need to really study up on the right size of everything. We need to maximize your profits on everything, so we'll take this like a puzzle. I'll call some friends and we'll get some estimates on some different things, and we'll sit down and look at it."

"This is exciting," she said, looking about.

"It is. This is a great piece of property. You've got water. You've got land that slopes, where it's good drainage. You've got good grassy area, and then you've got the more barren area. You've got a great combination of things that can grow different things. We need to look into the viability of prickly pear cactus. I'm not sure that there's a big of a call for that or if it's just more of a, you know, smaller type thing. It might not be something that would be worthwhile, but we can look into it."

"I can hardly believe this is going to happen." She

couldn't help it as she grinned at him. They had made it through their first night. It had been awkward, but he had gone to his room, which he said was perfectly fine. And she'd gone to her room. And they hadn't come out until this morning for breakfast. It was funny how they were both up about the same time. They had coffee together while she fried up some bacon and eggs, and he went outside and fed her goats for her. She'd watched him through the window and her heart had squeezed a little, watching him. She had to admit it was pleasant having someone here in the mornings but reminded herself that eventually, after she got this place going and profitable, that then she could think about finding a husband. The one right for her.

But right now, looking at him, he was like her angel. He had come to help her, save her land and when he left, she was going to have a business. It was amazing.

She had told Dixie that she was going to be quitting because they were going to be working on the business, and she didn't need to be taking her time away. While he was here working, he had told her that she didn't need to work; they would get it all figured out. So she was going to work for the next two weeks, but Dixie wouldn't hear of it.

Dixie was keeping her secret; she knew they had gotten married. And until it was out everywhere, she didn't want to let everybody in on it. Dixie had thought they had a whirlwind romance. It was kind of weird thinking about people's wrong idea—she was lying to them, basically. Not being in town for people to ask her about it was easier; actually, hiding out here between Blanco and Stonewall distanced her from town, which was a good thing. No questions.

"So where will the cows go? Probably up closer to the house, you think. Or will the cattle be better out here? I'm just not real sure about all that since I never thought about just doing calves."

"I think it will be better to have the calves closer to the barn. Kind of like you do your goats. Might even have to get you a donkey to put out there with the calves—you know, to protect them from coyotes and things."

"That's right, I forgot that donkeys do that. I see

donkeys in pastures all the time and forget what they're there for. Forgot that they actually serve a purpose and aren't just there 'cause they're cute."

He laughed. "From what I understand, they're not really cute and they're not always tame. They can be pretty mean. A good ole hard kick from a donkey will send a coyote running for cover."

"Yeah, makes me like them all the more, so I think I'd kind of like having a donkey. I'll have goats and a donkey and calves and chickens. I'll just be a regular old McDonald."

He smiled. "You'd be a very pretty old McDonald. And your farm will be very successful, I think."

She felt warm all over at his compliment. They walked back toward the truck. "Have you told any of your family yet that we've gotten married?" It had been something she had been wondering about ever since yesterday. She had known that he hadn't told his grandfather because he hadn't wanted to give his grandfather the satisfaction. He wanted him to find out whenever he found out but not from him. She felt weird about him and his grandfather kind of being on the outs, especially when the wedding was such a blessing to her.

"Not yet, but I plan to tell them—probably today. I just wanted to get here and get settled in and you and me to get comfortable with each other before I have anybody starting to ask me questions and all that."

"Okay. You think it will be okay...I mean, with them?"

"Oh, they'll be great with it. They kept telling me I needed to do it and I just wouldn't. I mean, I was so mad at Granddaddy that I was determined I wasn't going to do it. But thankfully, Todd knew what to say to me, and I'm looking at it with different eyes right now." His gaze warmed as he looked at her.

* * *

They had been married a week and a half when Beck walked around the corner of the barn looking for Mollie Mae. He had flown today and the whole time he had been in flight, his thoughts had been on his wife— Mollie. Living in the same house with Mollie Mae was turning out to be a little harder than he had thought. He found the woman irresistible in the mornings, in long, sloppy pajama bottoms and a big T-shirt. She had come out of the bedroom groggy, her hair a mess, and looking grouchier than he had ever believed possible. The woman was not a morning person. He had started making sure he had a pot of coffee made for her when she woke up just because...well, just because he liked seeing the pleasure that came across her face when she realized all she had to do was accept the coffee mug he held out to her instead of having to make the coffee herself and wait for it to brew in the morning.

Yeah, he had gotten to where he had really enjoyed seeing that part of her. It was like one sip and she transformed, kind of like those commercials where the person was a grouch and then, when they took one bite of a chocolate bar, they turned into their regular lovable self. Yup, that was Mollie and coffee, and he loved to watch the transformation.

But that wasn't just it; he enjoyed working with her. They were working side by side, coming up with a plan, and he had to fight leaning close because she had that smell that just drove him bonkers. He didn't know what it was, but it was a combination of something that she put together—maybe it was her hair shampoo and her conditioner mixed. Somebody had come up with an unforgettable scent in a bottle if that was what that unique scent was that she wore.

But, anyway, it was becoming a torture. He didn't want to mislead her. He didn't want to take advantage of her while they were married as far as kissing her or ever taking their relationship past where it was now because when they split up at the end of three months, they needed to walk away free and clear. He wanted to have no regrets and that meant not worrying about whether or not he had been honorable during this marriage. But that didn't mean he wasn't suffering. He was attracted to his wife more than he had ever dreamed possible. Every day that he was in her presence, it became deeper and deeper, the hole that he had dug for himself.

Today, he couldn't find her. He had been home for twenty minutes and had yet to find her. He decided she must be out feeding the goats. He hadn't looked around there yet. He had looked at the garden. He had looked at the chicken house. He had even looked at the water well house. Finally, he had realized she was probably playing with her goats. She loved those goats.

What he wasn't expecting when he rounded the corner was to see Mollie Mae Talbot McCoy's rounded rump sticking out of one of the smaller little goat houses that they had built for the babies.

He'd had the bright idea that maybe the baby goats would like something to play in like the adults had when it came to the concrete culverts that they walked around in, sat in, rolled around in, climbed on. He had made some smaller versions, but that had only one end open; the other was closed in case the baby goats wanted to go inside and sleep. Baby goats were small—even smaller than Mollie, who was thin but obviously too big for the small house. She wiggled her rump. He cocked his head to one side and watched with interest. He couldn't help it. She had on a pair of cutoff jeans that covered her rear quite nicely. He heard her grumble. She yanked but remained where she was. And then it dawned on him—she was stuck.

Walking up with a mixture of concern and humor, he cleared his throat.

"I didn't realize I built it for you. I thought it was for baby goats."

She paused in her wiggling.

"Thank goodness you're here. I've been stuck for about thirty minutes. I cannot get out. My little goat is in here and she would not come out, so I thought I would reach in here and get her out. But my arms just couldn't quite reach her because you made it so long. And I don't know what's wrong. My rib cage—it won't let me out."

That was really curious. "Did you squeeze in somehow to get your ribs in? I'm not sure I understand how you can get in and then not get out."

"I'm not either." Her voice was slightly muffled from being inside the container. "But I guess maybe because I sucked my gut in and I was able to go in forward and squeeze in but now I keep catching on my rib cage."

"Seriously?" He hated to be redundant, but it was really odd.

"Seriously. I'm stuck. Beck, can you get me out of here? And the baby goat's terrified. She doesn't know what to think about me being in here with her. And it's dark. Thankfully, there's no snakes in here with us—I did check on that before I crawled in."

As if for emphasis, she wiggled and yanked and then groaned because obviously it hurt.

"Okay, hold on. I can get you out of there, I think."

"What do you mean, you think?"

"I'm going to have to go get my tools and come back. I'll take the front off first. Then we'll have to take off a piece of wood one at a time until we get to the ones surrounding your body. On the side there." It would be simple enough, but it sounded complicated. It was like a little doghouse and the sides just needed to come apart.

"Okay, but please hurry. I've been in this position for so long, I'm starting to feel a little bit dizzy."

"Well, there's always that if you faint maybe you'll be so relaxed, I'll be able to pull you out by your feet."

She kicked out, trying to kick him. "I better not pass out."

He laughed. "I'll be right back." He headed to the barn, grabbed his tools, and came back. Within just a few minutes, he had the first board off on the right side. The only problem was every time he had to hit to get the nail out, she groaned. So obviously she wedged herself in there good. He couldn't help but remark on that. "Don't you know to never squeeze yourself into a spot because you always have to figure out how to get yourself out?"

"You are not helping," she growled, making him chuckle.

"You are really testy. For a little thing, you have some punch."

"I'm going to punch you," she said, sounding as harmless as a feather.

"I like a lady who likes to brawl." He could imagine her shaking her head inside. He might be in for a good whack across the arm when she got out. Finally, he got the board off and she sat up and rubbed her rib cage.

"I don't know what I'd done if you hadn't come along," she said.

"I'm glad I came home. So maybe these aren't a good idea. Somebody else or maybe one of the big goats could get stuck in there."

"Maybe we'll just leave this one side off. I don't plan to be crawling in there again." As she talked, the little baby goat bounced out, hopped right in her lap, and snuggled.

"At least you got the goat out."

She smiled up at him. "Did anybody ever tell you, Beck McCoy, that you're a smart aleck?"

He chuckled. "I've been told that a lot. My brothers love to tell me that and I've made Caroline about as aggravated as you are right now, too. Only problem is she let me have it. You tried to kick me, but she would have met the aim on purpose. Or punch me in the bicep."

"Well, I'm seriously thinking about it. I think you found a lot of joy looking at me stuck in there."

He gave her an *I-can't-lie* look. "I have to admit, I couldn't complain about the view. You, Mollie Mae, have a very nice figure, may I say."

She did punch him then, right in the calf.

He laughed. "Okay, now you're getting violent on me."

"Thank you very much for getting me out but I have to say, I am a little shocked by how much you seemed to enjoy that."

"Don't get me wrong. I'm in this marriage to get a blessing out of it for both of us. But I am a man and you are a woman, and I'd be lying if I told you this wasn't hard. You are..." *What was he saying?* His thoughts of her all afternoon were getting out of hand. He never meant to say anything like that to her, never meant to let her know how he was thinking of the situation they were in. He hadn't expected this little interlude, either.

She looked at him, the color in her face getting normal now.

Her expression grew serious. "I would be lying if I didn't tell you I'm having a little bit of the same issue, so it's good to know that I'm not the only one suffering in this relationship."

"Really?" *Why did that admission from her make*

him feel so stinking good?

She stood and dusted off the front of her shirt, which drew his attention to the rest of her figure. Then he quickly looked away, to her face.

"So I guess now that we've got that little bit of information off our chest, we'll just lock it away and pretend like we didn't have that conversation. How does that sound?"

"Sensible."

He stood and gathered his tools. "Fine. Then I'll go put my tools up. And then I'll go unload my truck. I brought some supplies for the irrigation system out at the peach orchard. I thought we could take the tractor out and dig some trenches."

She nodded and they continued to stare at each other. An uncomfortable moment passed between them. He was tempted to ask her whether she was reconsidering their business deal and wanting to add a little pleasure in there. *Maybe just a kiss.* Then he said, *nope*, shook himself out of his stupidity, and walked away. Walking away was the best thing he could do right now.

CHAPTER TWELVE

Mollie helped Beck lay the rows of pipe for the irrigation in the peach orchard. They had been working for a couple of hours and even though it was evening now, it was still sweaty business on the hot Texas day. And dirty.

She was a dirty, gritty mess and probably completely unattractive. Why was she thinking about being attractive or unattractive? Well, of course, it was because of the conversation that they had had earlier while she had been stuck in the goat house. What a ridiculous situation she had gotten herself into—and then the conversation they had with her admitting that she was having trouble with thoughts of him and of their situation.

Yup, living with Beck McCoy had proved to be quite an ordeal. The man looked far too good in the morning for her to be anything but grumpy when she got up. She was trying, but when she had to come out of her room, already knowing he was going to look better than any man had a right to look in the morning, all perky and happy, all muscled and fresh out of the shower, well...it was just too much to bear.

Just the thought of seeing him put her in more of a sour mood than she normally was in the morning. And he thought she was just normally like that.

He had no idea.

Thankfully, he was a blessed spirit and had realized that coffee helped, so when he would hand her that mug, it did help her get a grip on her emotions. It had only been a week and a half. She wished she was still working at the diner. At least when she went into the diner, she had had a place to de-stress as she waited on the customers.

But she wasn't working there any longer since Dixie told her she could hire a new waitress who had applied already.

That meant she was with Beck most of the time. And she could admit to herself that some of her favorite times were sitting on the porch in the evening with him, watching the sun set as they talked about what they were going to do to her little farm.

She stared at what they had done so far to the peach orchard. He had had a company come out on his second day at the ranch and they planted all these peach trees. There were a hundred of them. Her ranch was more a farm now, and she loved it.

He hadn't had them put in the irrigation—said that was simple and they could do it. And so they were. It was easy to tell Beck enjoyed working with his hands; he enjoyed hard labor. The guy might be a billionaire, he might enjoy flying planes all over the place for his elite clientele, but Beck McCoy was no slouch when it came to getting in the trenches and working hard. It came naturally to him.

"Who taught you to work like you do?" she asked now, swiping at a fly that had decided it was in love with her.

"Same as who taught you to work like you do—

my granddaddy taught me like your granddaddy taught you."

Why did grime look good on him and made flies love her? "Yes, he did." She sighed. "I miss him."

Beck leaned back on his boots. His knees were in the dirt because this work required you to be on your knees in the dirt. "Yeah." He took his glove off and reached for his hat. He fanned her then himself for a minute as he studied their handiwork. "I miss my granddaddy too. But there's not much I can do about that."

"Don't you think you should go see him?"

"Nope. He knows where to find me. I called Cal, his lawyer. Cal informed him that we were married, so he knows that I'm doing what he wanted me to do. He knows my time clock is ticking. He knows that in two months and two weeks, give or take a few days, I'll be home free. I'll be my own man and he won't be able to do this to me again."

Why did his words stab so hard at her? He couldn't wait for their time together to end and she had to keep reminding herself that, or she would be so easily tempted to make more out of the situation than was there. She was in a dangerous situation, which she had been thinking all along—but every day, it grew worse. However, when he made statements like this, it hurt but it helped.

"And I'll be home free, too, with a great-looking place and an income of my own, all because of you. I guess we better get more done, because we have a lot more to do once we get this peach orchard growing."

He grinned at her. "You are a hard boss. Let me get a drink of water. You need to get one, too, and then we'll get on the next row."

She stood and walked toward the truck; he followed. She picked up her water bottle and took a long swig. It had a little salty taste to it, which was something Beck taught her to do. "Put a little pinch of salt in your water and it will help keep your energy up." She'd gotten used to the taste and he was right—it did help with her energy.

One more thing she learned from Beck McCoy.

One more thing that would stay with her long after he was gone.

* * *

The next couple of weeks passed. And it was getting harder by the day to keep her head straight. Beck was wonderful. He was working, flying an airplane, then coming back and helping her make this ranch into her dream spot. On the flip side, the reality was...he wasn't going to be here in the end.

She kept having to remind herself of that fact so she would pull back. But then she would hand him a pipe or a mug of coffee, a glass of tea, just so his fingers would brush against hers and her heart would go crazy. Yes, her heart. She needed to have a conversation about her heart. Her heart was having problems—running her ragged as it raced like an Olympian runner exploding out of the starting blocks over and over again.

And now tonight, it was a whole new kind of stress. His brothers and their wives and Caroline and her husband were coming to have dinner with them. Also, his cousins and their wives were joining them too. Everyone but his grandfather.

She filled up the tea pitcher and looked out the window. Beck was flipping ribs on the brand-spanking new, super-duper beautiful BBQ pit he had put on her tiny back deck. It looked as out of place there as she felt in his house. But he had said everybody needed a BBQ pit, despite the fact that she had never barbequed in her entire life. If she wanted BBQ, she bought it from someone who knew what they were doing—that not being herself.

Beck assured her he would teach her how to use the huge grill. But he didn't get it…why would she use that big thing for just herself after he was gone? A picture instantly popped into her mind of her attempting to BBQ for herself on the porch, alone and missing him. It was a pathetic thought.

So was having a bunch of billionaires here in her small home. She told herself over and over again to hold her head up and not think about it because, well, Beck didn't. Beck never said anything bad about her place. He actually acted as if he loved her place. But then again, he also said he was really comfortable in the little bed in the guest room where he slept, and she knew that was not the truth. His long legs had to hang off the end of that short bed and the mattress was ancient and lumpy. Then there was the fact that her grandmother had decorated it something like thirty years ago with lots of floral wallpaper—pink roses that now had a yellowing tint to them. And then there was the mismatched bedcover of yellow roses...maybe if the pink roses had another forty years to yellow, the wall and the bedcover would match.

Needless to say, Beck was a completely good sport and hadn't even cringed when she'd led him into that floral explosion that first night. He'd said it reminded him of his grandmother and he'd slept very well. She kind of doubted that his grandmother had put that many flowers on the wall. She had probably had an interior decorator come in and fix up their guest rooms. She had thought one day maybe she would decorate but the money had just never been there, nor the time.

They hadn't seen his family since they got married. She knew Beck had told them to give them some time and she knew that he hadn't seen his granddaddy yet. That worried her. She wished he would. She didn't understand his grandfather, but she hated there was a rift between them. She missed her granddaddy fiercely and she understood Beck being angry. But still, it was his granddaddy, and he was alive. That was something to cherish and not waste time with anger.

If she could have one more day, just one more day with her sweet granddaddy, she would tell him how much she loved him and she would just sit with him, hold his hand, and have a conversation. Tears sprang to her eyes thinking about it. It was those kinds of things that people didn't think about until it was too late.

She was very thankful that she and her granddaddy had not been angry at each other…she was actually thankful she hadn't known the state of things before he'd died so that there had been no reason for her to even know she should be angry.

Weird but true.

She blinked hard, breathed deeply, and focused on the gorgeous male specimen that God had sent her to help fix the mess she was in. She did not need to cry before the billionaires arrived. The last thing she needed was to greet them with a red nose and eyes. No, it was time to make a peach cobbler.

That was her granddaddy's favorite. She kind of thought she could have done something a little more fancy for all of Beck's family who was coming, but something about having something her granddaddy loved comforted her. It was as if serving her granddaddy's favorite dessert was like he was there with her. Very quickly, she opened a box of yellow cake mix and mixed it together just like the directions said—the eggs and a little bit of oil and water—and then she poured it into a Pyrex pan. Then she opened up a can of peaches and poured them on top. She sprinkled a good helping of cinnamon and brown sugar over that. It was going to be wonderful and she already felt better as she slid it into the oven.

Soon the house would smell delicious, another good reason to cook this particular dessert. When Beck's family walked into her tiny home, they would immediately breathe in that scent and that was probably all they would be able to think about, it was so delicious smelling. Maybe they wouldn't see how worn everything was, and the cracked Sheetrock, and different things she had just gotten used to over the years. Beck had even had to buy brand-new lawn chairs for the back deck so everybody would have a place to sit. He'd called her from the store when he had stopped on his way back from flying and asked her what color she wanted.

Her little house was white with black trim, so she had thought maybe some red would look good. It was bright and cheery back there. But she nibbled at her lip and wondered whether maybe it would have been better to buy a muted color, like a tan or a brown. *Did the bright color say that she wasn't refined?*

"Suck it up, buttercup," she muttered. "You're not refined. You're a country girl living in a country house, and that's all there is to it."

She was having these reservations as she hurried to the bedroom to change clothes before everybody arrived.

"You're only in his life temporarily and you need to remember that," she told the woman in the mirror.

"Thanks for keeping me straight. And keeping me honest."

With that, she strode back into her bedroom and yanked on her boots. Out here, boots were the thing and, well, she hadn't had time to do her toenails, and she certainly wasn't going to wear flip-flops with bad toenails in front of these people. Not when she knew that all the girls in his family probably spent a whole lot of money at spas and things, getting their nails professionally done. She had never even set foot in a spa. *Enough of that.* She was done feeling sorry for herself. *It was ridiculous, and it wasn't becoming.*

She went back in the kitchen. That dessert smelled delicious. She reached down and looked in the oven. Just a few more minutes and it would be ready. She went over to the refrigerator, pulled out a tray of ice, twisted it, and let the ice fall into a bowl. Beck had bought some crushed ice for later; it was in an ice chest out on the deck. But right now, she just used the ice they had in her ancient refrigerator as she filled two glasses with ice then poured some sweet tea into them. She walked outside. *Yes, she was crazy.* She was flirting with fire as she smiled at Beck.

"Hey there—you look nice. I'm anxious for everyone to come and get to meet you."

His words were like bombs to her aching heart. She held the glass out to him and he took the tea. His fingers brushed hers, just as she'd known they would. A thrill raced up her arms and settled in her heart; her stomach tilted and her knees went weak. And of course, there were palpitations. She was a wreck.

She smiled, admitting that she enjoyed the sensation. She logged it in her memory for when he would be gone, and she wouldn't feel his touch anymore. "Thought you might like some sweet tea. It sure does smell good out here."

"I hope you like it. It's my granddaddy's recipe. You know, I might be at odds with him but my granddaddy knows how to make BBQ. So that's what we're having tonight."

"I'm glad. I think you need to see your granddaddy and maybe make peace with him. I'm kind of doing that, too. I've made my granddaddy's special peach cobbler, so we'll have a little bit of both of them with us tonight."

"That peach cobbler smells amazing. Are we having Blue Bell with it too?" he asked, bypassing conversation about his granddaddy.

"Is there any other way to have hot peach cobbler?"

"Not in my book, there isn't. If it's not too much trouble, you may have to make one of those for the two of us that I don't have to share with my family."

"That's the beauty of it—it's very simple. Just like me and my granddaddy. It's really economical, too, so he always kept the ingredients on hand. He blamed his little poochy belly on it." She laughed, thinking about Granddaddy. "He'd tease about the little pooch on his belly all the time. He'd worked hard all his life, and I felt like if he wanted to eat some peach cobbler and Blue Bell, more power to him."

"I agree." Beck smiled at her as he sipped his tea. "You know, you make the best tea I've ever tasted."

She smiled at his words, pleased. "That's from my grandma. I don't take credit for anything. I only do what they taught me. She could make the best tea in

Texas."

"Well, she passed it on to you very well. I'm probably going to have a little pooch myself by the time I leave here from eating your peach cobbler and drinking your sweet tea."

She couldn't help it; her gaze shot to his six-pack abs. Those hard abs she'd felt a time or two when they were dancing, or they were working, and her hand had accidentally touched his stomach while they were passing fence post or PVC pipe. It would take a lot of peach cobbler and a lot of sweet tea to make that man have a pooch on his belly. She actually didn't care. The reality—the dangerous reality—was she would take Beck McCoy any way she could get him, pooch or no pooch.

CHAPTER THIRTEEN

"She's really a nice woman." Wade sat beside Beck, against the railing of the deck.

Todd agreed from where he sat in one of the red lawn chairs that they had put on the deck. "Yeah. And golly, that peach cobbler was amazing."

"I have to agree with them," his brother Ash said. "You did good when you found somebody to marry. And here all this time you've been griping about the whole issue."

Morgan also sat in one of the red chairs. The fire pit he had purchased when he had bought the BBQ pit sat between them, and even though it was a summer night, they had lit it just for the atmosphere. "Don't you think that it's not as terrible as you thought it would be?" he asked. "I mean, I totally understand it. I remember standing on the lava rocks in Kauai, thinking what a miserable lot Granddaddy had dealt me, and then next thing I know, there's Amber out there nearly drowning. If I hadn't been standing on those rocks, I don't know what would have happened to her. I might have lost her and never even known what I'd missed. Makes me sick thinking about it. Are you and Mollie giving this a real shot?"

Denton, leaning against the opposite railing, squinted at him in the evening sunshine. "You can look around this deck here and see that none of us thought we would find somebody to marry us, much less actually falling in love. But if it hadn't been for Granddaddy, we wouldn't be this happy."

Beck's hand tightened on the long-handled grilling fork, his thoughts in turmoil. "Mollie is a great lady. I wouldn't have married her if I was going to have a terrible time during the three months. But she's been through a lot. I'd be stupid to not be attracted to her and I'm pretty protective of her, too, but those two things don't mean love and that's not what we agreed on. We agreed that we would marry and then we would go our separate ways. We're friends, though I like her a lot."

"You're probably like I was," Todd said. "I wasn't going to stay with Ginny no matter what, just because I was determined that Granddaddy wasn't going to tell me what to do. That's probably what you're thinking, isn't it?"

"I've thought that. And I have to say that I feel real strongly about that."

Jesse, who had been silent, spoke up. "Beck, just remember, in the end, if you don't love her with your whole heart, y'all need to split up so you can both find the love of your lives. I think this talk is dangerous, encouraging you to fall in love. Because only your heart can do that."

Beck liked Jesse. Jesse had always been level-headed, and he was glad that Jesse and Caroline had found their way to each other.

"Thanks, Jesse. I agree with you. Mollie deserves someone to love and adore her with all of their heart, and I would never stand in the way of that. I'm not going to stay because I'm not going to take advantage of her emotions."

He'd been thinking about that. They were struggling; it was harder and harder not to reach out and touch her every morning. They used the excuse of their fingers touching when they passed glasses between each other, like the tea earlier and the coffee in the mornings. Or when they worked together, and he'd brush past her too close because he just wanted to feel that spark of sensation that he only felt when he was close to her. But that wasn't love and he knew it. And he was going to have to keep reminding himself that Mollie deserved the best of everything.

The door opened then, and all the ladies strolled out. It was a great group. They all barely fit on that deck, but they made it. All the women took a chair beside their man, and Mollie looked a little bit out of place as she watched his brothers take the hands of their wives.

Caroline sat in Jesse's lap, put her arms around him, and kissed him on the lips. "I have missed you, even though we were only gone for a little while."

"I missed you, too. But I had to give your brother a little talking-to about putting so much sauce on his BBQ. Or he's going to cause me to gain weight. And I have to keep looking good or you might run away with some handsome stranger. Maybe the UPS guy. He sure does show up a lot around our place."

She laughed. "Oh yeah, me and the UPS guy, we're close. I think you're right—you know, in those little brown shorts, he's got some mighty nice-looking legs. But sorry, I know beneath those blue jeans you've got some great legs, too. We might need to get you a little sun on them, though."

Laughter erupted around the deck and Beck took that moment to pat the railing beside him. Mollie walked over and leaned back against it. He moved his arm behind her on the railing and let his hand brush her arm. They weren't holding hands but at least she was in the shelter of his body. And he could smell that wonderful scent that included the vanilla she had used in that wonderful peach cobbler.

"They didn't scare you off in there, did they?" he asked softly.

She turned her head slightly to him and whispered, "No, they're great. They were looking at pictures of Granddaddy and me. And my grandma."

"You two sure are quiet over there. What are y'all talking about?" Ginny asked.

He wondered whether Mollie had realized that Ginny was pretty outspoken. She spoke her mind and sometimes she embarrassed people.

"We were wondering if y'all want to take a tour," he said. "We can take the ATV and a couple of trucks, and we can drive out to see the peaches. And you've got to see the baby goats."

The gals all squealed when they heard "baby goat" and within moments, he had successfully gotten everybody off the deck and standing around, looking at goats.

The goats put on a good show, jumping and bobbing. Then everyone rode out to the peach farm. It would be a few years before they had peaches—probably three—but he was proud of what they were doing. He envisioned what it was going to look like around here when they were finished. All the different streams of income Mollie would have. It was a good feeling.

Mollie looked proud as she walked through the field, telling everyone about the peaches and what kind they were and how thrilled she was. He liked watching her and that warm feeling filled him that he got when he looked at her. Mollie Mae Talbot McCoy was goodness, all wrapped up in a nice package.

"Beck," Caroline came over to him, "you do remember about the charity ball we're supposed to go to in Austin?"

"It slipped my mind."

"Well, I think that you should go and bring Mollie. She would enjoy it. It would give you two more to do than work. Work and no play makes Beck a dull boy. Plus, I told Mollie she could come to the spa with all of us. We're all going day after tomorrow as a treat before the benefit, but she said no. However, I have not given up. I am enlisting your help. It would be good for her. I don't think she gets treats very often and as hard as that girl works, she deserves a bunch. Convince her to join us, okay? We'll take her shopping, too. We're all using this as an excuse to get new dresses. Yes, I know, I don't need an excuse, but the others do." She smiled. "It's actually a bonding thing we woman do, and we'd love to treat Mollie and bond with her at the same time. And then you get the bill and the treat of seeing her all dolled up on date night. Put in a good word for us, and we'll pick her up in the limo."

He glanced over at where Mollie was talking to Allie, who had left her babies with her housekeeper who loved keeping them. Holly hadn't brought her babies either; she had actually left them with Granddaddy because he had loved playing with the great-grandbabies. His housekeeper had stayed to help, just in case he needed an extra hand. Out of all of the sisters-in-law who were there, Mollie reminded him somewhat of Allie because she was soft-spoken, and yet sometimes, she had some fire in her that he enjoyed.

He could only imagine her dressed up in a fancy dress, and suddenly he realized he wanted to see Mollie all dressed up. "You send the car by. I'll make sure she's ready. I think that's a good idea."

"Great. And you make sure you dress up, too, because I'm afraid being stuck out here on this farm might be cramping y'all's style."

He laughed. "You could be right."

* * *

After everyone left, Mollie went into the kitchen that was already clean because all the girls had insisted on helping before they went out and joined the guys on the deck earlier. Her small kitchen had been full, but it had been fun working together, washing and drying and putting away dishes. And then they'd had time to chat. When Caroline had told her that there was an upcoming charity ball that they were all expected to go to, her heart had just fallen to her feet. She had nothing to wear to a charity ball, and it was something so out of her league that she had told them no. Especially when they had told her that they were all going to go to the spa and that they would come by and pick her up in the limo. But it didn't stop there. They were all going shopping for dresses after the spa and they'd help her pick out a dress.

She had told them she had to work with Beck that day and that if Beck had to go to the ball, he could go without her. They all told her they wanted her to go and several of them told her that becoming a McCoy took some getting used to at first. But they had all finally gotten used to it and were adjusting, and she would too. But she didn't tell them that in the end she wasn't going to be a McCoy. When this was all said and done, she was going to take back her family name, the name that fit her—Mollie Mae Talbot. Someone who didn't need to wear evening dresses and get spa days and buy fancy shoes and go to balls.

She had enjoyed them, though. They were all so nice, and she had to admit that she had kind of misjudged all of them. They had been gracious and really picked out so many special places in her house and commented on them, like the quilt that her grandmother had made and was lying over the back of the old couch. It was beautiful and her grandmother had hand stitched every stitch. Allie had noticed that, and then Caroline had noticed the photos on the wall of her and her granddaddy. She had commented how similar some of them were to pictures she had with her and her granddaddy. And she talked about the boys on the ranch that she and Jesse lived with—her boys, as she called them. She was making sure that she took a lot of photos of them and covered the walls in the main entrance with those pictures because memories came from photos.

She'd said that photos told the story of a life well lived. Mollie loved that. Mollie really liked Caroline. And then each of the others had commented on something: her goats, her peach orchards, the yellow color of her dishes. They'd all been so generous and kind, and they had all loved her granddaddy's peach cobbler. There was absolutely none of it left and she thought that Todd and Denton were going to fight over the last bite, just a small portion that was left in the bowl. In the end, it had been Ginny who had swept over while they were playfully bickering over it and scooped the piece out with her spoon and swallowed it before they could even realize what she had done.

Ginny was a hoot. She was funny and tart and she was exactly who Mollie wished she could be when she grew up. She laughed. She *was* all grown, and there was no way she would ever be the type of character that Ginny was. She was kind; she was sarcastic; she said what she meant. Sometimes it was with a sarcastic comment, but she was very likable and fun. And she had told her that when they had tried to get her to go on a spa day, they had almost had to drag her. Still, even after that, Mollie had declined.

She just felt too uncomfortable. New things did not come easy to her. And most of them didn't realize that it had mostly been her and her granddaddy all these years. To think about going to a fancy spa and getting all dolled up to go to a fancy ball, like Cinderella, it might just be too much for her to handle. 'Cause she might get to thinking that Beck was her prince. Something that she was still having to tamp down inside her. Nobody understood the tightrope she was walking.

Beck came in from where he had gone out to check on a baby calf that he and his brothers had been talking about. He looked so good, so handsome.

"How is it?"

"It's going to be okay. Ash took a look and said it wasn't serious. He said he thought a coyote had gotten after it. I think it's time to find us a donkey. I know somebody over near the Enchanted Rock who has a few, so maybe we can go pick one out."

"I'd like that. I love the Enchanted Rock. I love that area."

"Yeah, I do, too. We can hike up it, if you want." The big pink dome that rose up out of the countryside outside of Fredericksburg was an unusual rock and an easy walk for most people. It was a cool thing to do.

"If you want to."

"I do. That's what we can do—we'll pack a lunch and we'll hike up there and have us a little picnic. And then we'll hike down. You and I should be able to hike that easy."

"I like that idea." This was more her style instead of a fancy ball.

"Then let's do it." He walked over and leaned against the counter and crossed his arms. Their shoulders touched.

She had wondered why he'd gotten so close. She liked it. She had been wanting to be close to him all night. "I like your family. You should be very proud."

"I do like them a lot. And they're all so happy."

"They all seem to be. And all those babies are coming. And I'm sure more are going to happen before long because they just look too happy to not be making babies. You know what I mean." *Had she really said that?* She felt her cheeks go hot pink—she figured because she felt hot pink.

He looked at her, his eyes twinkling. "I think you're probably right. They probably are practicing making babies. And they're married, so they have every right to do that." His voice trailed off as his gaze dropped to her lips.

She bit her bottom lip as nervous energy rattled through her. *They were married, too.* Her cheeks burned at the thought. She didn't need to be thinking about that.

They weren't married like *that*.

But when he looked at her...holy moly, she could

only wish.

"My family likes you a lot. You were great tonight." He turned to face her.

"I like them." Her heart fluttered and then went into panic mode, skipping beats and bouncing all around like a baby goat on a sugar high.

Slowly, he reached his hand up and lightly brushed her cheek and then her jaw. And then, as her knees went weak, he tilted her chin and he kissed her. She hadn't expected that; she was probably going to pass out as his gentle kiss pulled a longing out of her that was in no way calm or collected. It was like a firestorm and like that first night when she had lost her ever-lovin' mind and thrown herself at him. She pretty much lost control. She slid her arms around his neck and held on like he was a life preserver.

He deepened the kiss, tugging her closer where their bodies met. Emotions and feelings that were pretty much new to her took over. She floundered in an ocean of emotions and was swept away with the current passion as she slid her fingers into his hair and she felt his fingers sliding into her hair.

This was what she'd waited her whole life to find. To feel.

Finally, he pulled away. Both of them were breathing hard and he looked like a guy who was torn between right and wrong. She understood it because she was right there with him. She wanted to take this moment and be a married couple in every sense of the vows. Wanted to pretend that they were going to be together forever, that they were in love...and that she wasn't just dreaming all this.

"Mollie Mae," he whispered against her lips then pulled back. "You're the sweetest person I've ever met. And you kiss like an angel. And I couldn't help kissing you and thanking you for making my family feel so comfortable tonight."

That had been a thank-you kiss. He was thanking her for being nice to his family. She gave a small smile. And hoped her voice sounded halfway natural. "It was my pleasure."

"I'm going to go to bed now. We have a date tomorrow to go pick out a donkey. And then to conquer the Enchanted Rock." He released her and stepped back.

She fought to appear unshaken. "Sounds perfect."

She watched him walk the distance to his door and without looking back, he went inside and shut it firmly behind him. She just stood there, dazed and very ashamed of herself. She had just jumped into that hook, line, and sinker—caved with just a mere touch of his lips. She was a marshmallow and she was burnt to a crisp right now.

She was going to bed, as soon as her legs would carry her.

Maybe she could read a book or listen to a book.

Maybe she could sleep. *Not happening.*

Maybe, if she were lucky, her brain would blank out everything that just happened, and she would not think about kissing Beck again.

Right—there was *no* wiping out that kiss.

It was all she could think about now.

CHAPTER FOURTEEN

The donkeys were cute and Mollie was instantly in love. Beck saw it in her face—her very expressive, lovely face.

Rufus, an old friend of the family, saw it too. The old guy winked at Beck in approval, and then the old cowboy grinned at Mollie. "Take your pick, little lady. These are all for sale. Which one do you feel drawn to?"

Mollie smiled at him and then walked over to a white-toned donkey that had been watching her with curiosity in its eyes.

Rufus spat out a stream of tobacco. "Well now, that there is Sally. She's as ornery a little creature as you'll find, but she's loyal. She's got a round kick, too, so if you're looking for something that might take care of some baby calves, she's a good choice. Now, if you're wanting a donkey that leads rope, then you might not want to pick that one. She's content to stay in the pasture and do her own thing but she doesn't like being told what to do."

Mollie smiled brightly. "Is that right, Sally?" She scratched Sally between the ears, and Sally closed her eyes, leaned her head to the side, and looked as if she were in heaven.

Rufus chuckled. "I believe you have found your donkey."

Mollie grinned. "Something about her just drew me to her. I believe she'll take care of my little calves. I'll be really grateful to her. I just still can't get over that a cute little donkey like this could do a round kick and knock a coyote out."

"Oh, she will. Don't make her mad and then walk behind her."

Beck frowned. "She better not."

Mollie shook her head. "I'll make sure to not make her mad."

"I was just kidding. She ain't going to kick you. But she'll take a coyote out in a second."

"Perfect." Mollie smiled at Rufus and then Beck.

Beck's mind slid back to the kiss in the kitchen the night before. He had hardly thought of anything else. That kiss had been a big, impulsive mistake.

When they had left, it was with an agreement that Rufus would deliver the donkey to them the next day. They drove to the Enchanted Rock and she talked excitedly about the donkey as they went.

The park was a pretty busy place this time of year. But it was a rock the size of a small town, so there was enough room for everyone. It was the weirdest rock he had ever seen: a big dome that people could just walk up at a gradual slope. It always looked to him like the moon had fallen from the sky and implanted itself in the ground, with half of it protruding from the earth. It was fascinating and made for a good outing.

He parked the truck and they got out. He got the picnic basket out and then, as they walked, he held his hand out. "I know it's a fairly easy walk but indulge me...just in case you slip. I don't want you to roll anywhere before I can get to you."

Her mouth fell open. "Maybe you should hang onto me in case *you* slip."

He laughed and then took her hand as she slipped it into his. The touch of her callused hand reminded him of why he was taking her on this picnic. He gently squeezed her hand, rough from the hard work she'd always done. He wanted to kiss those calluses and smooth them away. He wanted to make her life easier.

He laughed. "You do that. At least if we both roll down the hillside, we'll do it together."

"That sounds kind of fun, actually." She frowned. "I'm sorry I said that. When I'm around you, sometimes I say things that just totally shock me."

He laughed. "Speaking of, I shouldn't have kissed you last night. I'm doing things I shouldn't do too."

She breathed deeply, watching her step as they walked higher on the rock. "I gave in to it, too. I enjoyed it. To be honest, I've never really been kissed, so I've kind of enjoyed having my eyes opened about kissing, you know. After you leave, I'll be a little bit more prepared and experienced for when I start dating."

He missed his step and stumbled, then concentrated on putting one foot in front of the other. He didn't like thinking of her dating. *But could he say that to her?* This was temporary; they were getting a divorce. He couldn't tell her he didn't like the idea of her dating. *What kind of guy was he?* But he didn't like it. He didn't like it at all.

"You're getting a little assertive, I've noticed. Not exactly the quiet, timid girl I thought you were the night we met at the dance hall."

It was true. From that very first time she kissed him to her response to him on this last kiss, Mollie was surprising him in very pleasant ways. He put that thought out of his mind about how much he was enjoying kissing her. "If you're going to be in business for yourself, you're going to need to be more assertive, know what I mean?" *There, he had put it back on business terms, where they needed to be.*

She paused at a spot on the top of the dome and gazed out across the land that stretched out way below them. "I know what you're saying. And I'm glad about that, too. But you and I both know that I've been acting out of character when it comes to you and me. I've got to keep this business. But you tempted me with that kiss, and I just went a little crazy, so chalk it up as dating practice. Anyway, let's set up our picnic here. This is a great view."

"Yes, it is." He pulled his gaze off her and stared out over the land, welcoming the change of subject. He had things to talk to her about and there wasn't kissing involved.

He set the basket down. They spread the blanket out and then pulled out their lunch. Wasn't anything fancy—sandwiches, cold iced tea, some fruit that she had put in a container, and some cookies that she had made. He wasn't sure she knew it, but she was a good cook, and a good baker. Those cookies were great, but he knew if he complimented them, she'd tell him they were probably something her grandmother taught her to do and she didn't believe she deserved the praise. She always gave it to her grandmother or her granddaddy.

One thing he had learned about Mollie was she

was very humble. He liked that a lot. He wasn't sure whether it was humble or low self-esteem; he hoped it was just being humble because she was very good at a lot of things.

They settled on the blanket. His knee touched her knee and he liked the contact, even though he wasn't going to let himself dwell on that too much. But then again, he wasn't going to pull his knee away either. They watched the land below them, fields of Texas bluebonnets, cactus, and rolling grass that waved in the breeze. From way up here, it looked like it was a world away.

She smiled at him and pushed the hair out of her face that the wind had blown there. "Thanks for bringing me here. Brings back great memories."

"Me too. But I wanted to talk to you about something. It's about the charity ball. Caroline told me she'd mentioned it to you. But I hadn't mentioned it because I really hadn't planned on going."

"Why don't you like to go?"

"I'm not the guy who likes to dress up all that much, as you've probably realized. So sometimes I'll have a flight scheduled on dates like that and it helps me not have to go—you know when I have a flight I can't get out of."

"You do it on purpose then, just to get out of going?"

"That's right. But this year, I hadn't booked anything. It is good for me to be at some of these sometimes. It's good for the McCoy name and the McCoy brand. Sometimes a donation isn't enough, and I need to show up. And besides, this time I'd like to take you. I think you'd enjoy it. This one is nice. It's on a ranch near Austin instead of a hotel ballroom. There's a donor there who loves to host the benefit. They put up a big tent, with a great band and dinner and dancing. It will be fancy, don't get me wrong, but you'll like it. I told Caroline to come by for you in the limousine. You need some pampering and a day at the spa. And then going shopping with Caroline and the other girls will be fun for you."

She had put her sandwich down and bit that lip of hers, his gaze drawn instantly to her pretty pink mouth. He yanked his gaze off that mouth and the thoughts it had him thinking. Like how much he'd like to reach out right now and kiss her. "Is something wrong?"

"I really don't want to go. That's not a place for me."

"It's as much a place for you as it is for anybody." Her eyes shadowed and her gaze narrowed, and he saw an uncertainty there. "What's really bothering you?"

"That's what's bothering me. I don't belong there. I'm only going to be a McCoy for maybe two more months and then I'm not going to be a McCoy, so it's not a place for me. I don't have any fancy clothes. I barely ever wear high heels. It's just not me. There's really no reason for me to go through such an ordeal, putting myself out there in front of all those rich people who I really won't have anything in common with. What would I talk to them about?"

So that was it. He thought about his words carefully. "Mollie, you're just as good as anybody. You're probably one of the best people I've ever known. Just because they have money and you don't doesn't mean they're better than you. It certainly doesn't mean that I'm better than you. And I can promise you that none of my family thinks they're better than you."

She looked away and he hoped to goodness she wasn't going to cry. He wanted to keep speaking, trying to convince her, but he waited.

She looked back at him. "It might not be a good thing."

Unable to help himself, he reached up and pushed those strands of hair back off her face that the wind kept whipping across her cheeks. It was suddenly imperative she go with him. "Go with me. Please. I'll be right by your side the whole time. We'll dance— remember, we like to dance together. My family will be there. You'll have someone to talk to and nobody will think they're better than you. Go shopping with Caroline. My sister knows how to shop, and you'll have fun while they pamper you and fix you up with a beautiful dress. You'll feel like a princess, which is what I want you to feel like. You deserve it. And ignore the fact that in two months, we won't be married anymore. This is going to be fun, something for you to remember."

Only two months and then he was going to walk away from her, just like they had decided. His stomach felt hollow. His heart, too.

She raised her eyes to him, big pools of blue that he could just get lost in. Yeah, he was in a bad way, and he needed to talk to himself about that. Like Jesse said, he liked her very much, but this was about them going on with their lives and him getting out of her way so she could find the love of her life. Her soulmate.

She deserved to find someone out there one day who would be everything she ever dreamed of or wanted in a man. Someone who would love her deeply.

He wasn't ready for a commitment like that—wasn't sure when he would be, or if he would be. So he didn't need to be thinking thoughts about not being ready to let her go. He would let her go. But this night under the stars would be a great memory.

"Say yes." It was almost a command because he willed it in his heart so strongly.

She inhaled slowly. Her chest rose and then dropped as she let the breath out. Then she nodded.

"Okay, I'll go. But you better be right there, because when I start falling off my high heels, you'll need to catch me."

He smiled and let his hand run along her jaw, where he let his thumb roll across her chin. "I will be. I'll be right there by your side. As long as I'm around, I'm not going to let you fall."

Their gazes held and then she nodded. "Then you have yourself a date."

CHAPTER FIFTEEN

The spa day was amazing. Mollie decided that she was glad that Beck had talked her into coming. She might never do a spa day again but while she was part of the McCoy clan, the spa day was part of the treat that she had loved. The limousine was full of smiling McCoy women when it picked her up bright and early the next morning. They all welcomed her excitedly and then all began to talk about how other than Caroline, this had not been something they had ever been used to but now they loved to get together for girls' time.

Holly leaned back against the seat inside. "I was needing this. My babies aren't sleeping and even though Tess is nearly seven, the baby does tend to keep me awake most of the night. And Tess is very busy during the day, so life is pretty hectic. Poor Ash. His vet practice is so busy; he tries to help, but he's got his own hard nights with being called out to help sick livestock at night. So, this is going to be like heaven today. Ash said he was going to start sending me on more of them because he didn't want me getting too wore out. I think he wants to hire someone to come in a couple of days a week to help out. Isn't he sweet? But I don't know if I can let go enough to do it. But it's a nice thought. He's probably the sweetest man I've ever met." Her eyes got dreamy and she looked like a woman so very much in love.

Amber smiled. "That's kind of how I feel. I never traveled, never been around much of that at all, and now that I travel so much to these beautiful resorts with Morgan, I have to admit I tend to do spa treatments often. I mean, we're there and he tells me it's just part of the benefits, so I'm getting spoiled being a McCoy bride. But I love that man so. I'll take whatever perks I get from it."

Ginny slapped her leg, drawing their attention.

She grinned at Mollie. "I was too busy with my hands stuck in the dirt at my winery growing up, so I never even believed or thought I'd enjoy a massage. And then I met Todd and Caroline here who corrupted me with these beauty trips. I still have my hands in the dirt because I just love my vineyards, but it sure does feel nice having the kinks massaged out of my shoulders. And I'm pretty partial to those cucumber masks, too. Makes my skin feel so tingly. So, you just mark my words, Mollie, you're going to enjoy this. You might even get so used to it that you think maybe you and Beck have a future together."

Caroline patted her knee. "Don't look so panicked. We know you're not going to stay with Beck just because of what he offered you. I can tell you, none of these girls married my brothers and cousins for their money. Granddaddy set these weird guidelines up but the good Lord led us all together in perfect unions. And I know the money can be intimidating. My Jesse almost let it get in our way. Thankfully, it all worked out. I see the alarm in your eyes—relax. You just remember that if it's meant to be between you and

Beck, then open your heart and give it a chance, okay? Don't close it off. Now, let's enjoy the day. It will be fun, I promise."

She was a little bit in shock, thinking about everything they had said. She thought about Jesse and the fact that the money had almost kept him apart from Caroline. Later, as the masseuse rubbed her muscles until she felt boneless and all the tension eased out of her, she had a long time to think about her relationship with Beck. She knew she could or was falling in love with him; maybe she had already but she wasn't going to let herself admit it. And that was one of the things about this fairy-tale night they were going to have. It might make her heart want him too much.

It was worrisome but later, as they shopped and she stood in front of that mirror in the most beautiful ocean-blue dress that hung off her shoulders and swirled at her ankles, she blinked back tears. It was the most beautiful thing she had ever seen, and it even made her look…sophisticated. Oh, she knew that soon as the clock struck midnight at the end of her marriage contract, this beautiful fairy tale would disappear and she'd be back to where she'd been—she'd be better because Beck would make sure her place was beautiful and would help her make a living. But as far as she and Beck went, it would all be gone.

And yet, looking at herself in the mirror, her heart squeezed in hope that for that one night, there among the stars, she could have her dream fully. She'd embrace it and if Beck did too, she would be grateful. She didn't fit in with his life and she knew it. But maybe for just that night she could pretend she did.

* * *

While Mollie was at the spa, Sally the donkey got delivered to the house. Beck had been flying; he had had to fly to Washington State, so it had been a long day when he arrived home. He'd sent Caroline a text asking whether Mollie was enjoying herself, and Caroline had told him she'd relaxed and was having a great time.

That made him feel good, because he was worried about her. She was special and he wanted her to feel special. And he knew that his sister would make sure of it.

He spotted Sally and walked over to the fence to check on the donkey. It looked at him with eyes that said to stay back, so he didn't put his hand out. He wasn't in the mood to be bitten and he questioned buying the wild-eyed animal for a minute. Had he made a mistake bringing this donkey here for Mollie? Maybe the donkey letting Mollie pet it had been a fluke, a one-time deal, and it wasn't going to happen again. Maybe Sally didn't like being at a new place. He was worrying about that when the limo pulled up the drive.

Caroline waved at him from the window. "Hi, brother. I brought your wife back to you. I already dropped everyone else off and I'm not going to stay, but I just want to tell you we love this girl. We all had the best time. Anyway, come over here and help her get all her bags out because we loaded her up."

He laughed as he walked across the driveway to where the limousine driver was already out and opening the trunk. "You're going to have a lot of bags to carry in, sir. Do you want me to help you?"

Beck grinned. "Thanks, but I've got it." The trunk was full of bags. Mollie came over and stood beside him. She had left in jeans and a plaid shirt that he had seen her wear many times. And her boots. Now she had on a new pair of jeans that were rolled up at her ankles and a soft, pale-pink blouse that complemented her now tanned but slightly pink skin. It went well with her pretty blonde hair. And those sparkling blue eyes. He couldn't help but admire her. His first instinct was to bend down and give her a kiss. He fought off the instinct and reached for the bags.

"You look pretty."

"Thank you. I hope you don't mind. It is a lot. But Caroline made me do it. She just wouldn't take no for an answer."

He chuckled and planned to give Caroline a hug later for exactly doing what he had wanted her to do. "It's okay. I told her to do that. I told her to make sure you came home with anything that your heart desired. This is my treat for you today. Caroline came up with the idea but I wanted to do this."

"Well, you might not think that when you see your credit card bill. I tried not to look at the prices because I was getting sick in my stomach sometimes."

He couldn't help himself; he wrapped an arm around her, tugged her against him, and kissed her forehead. "Mollie, you are the nicest person I know, and I can see you getting sick at your stomach about that. But believe me, it's fine. If I can't spend this money on someone I want to spend it on, then there's no reason to have it."

She looked up at him and he wanted to kiss her again. *He had it bad.*

"Well, thank you. I'll help you carry it in so this nice man who was so kind to drive us around all day can get back home to his family. Thank you, Sam."

"You are very welcome."

"Thank you from me too." Beck slipped him a tip and then they unloaded the bags. Moments later, Caroline was waving out the back of the limo as it pulled out of the driveway, leaving him and Mollie and a big bunch of bags sitting all around them as they waved good-bye.

He looked at the bags after the limo was gone. There was one thing that wasn't a bag; it was a box and she told him her dress was in that box. She held up another bag that had some weird name that started with an L written across it.

"My heels. These shoes cost a ridiculous amount of money. Caroline said they looked uncomfortable but that I would be able to dance all night in them. And they'd make my legs look amazing." She laughed. "I'm glad they do something because I'm getting chills just holding the bag."

"I think your legs already look amazing, so I'll be eager to see them in the shoes."

Suddenly, a loud heehaw ripped through the air.

Mollie spun toward the pen. "Sally!" She set the bag back on the ground and jogged over to pet the waiting donkey.

The animal acted like a puppy as it cuddled with Mollie. Totally not the same animal that had greeted him—or *not* greeted him—earlier.

He had never seen anything like it before. The look that that donkey had given him was gone; in its place were the adoring eyes of Sally as she looked at Mollie. Mollie held her hand out and the donkey just laid its head in her palm.

"She's beautiful, isn't she? We're going to keep the baby calves up close here because I want to see this pretty little thing every day and I don't want her to get lonesome out there. If I want to go out there to pet her, I want her to be able to come to the fence and get all the petting she wants. This little donkey is like a puppy, she's so loving."

He snorted. "If you had seen the way she was looking at me a few minutes ago, you might not say that. I was beginning to wonder if we had made a mistake."

Mollie grinned at him. "We did not make a mistake. Sally is now a part of my family. And when you're gone, I'll have her and my baby goats to keep me company."

That idea did not agree with him. He wasn't thrilled anymore about the prospect of leaving her alone out here. His protective instincts had just kicked in too hard around her and he knew when he left, he was going to be worried about her all the way out here by herself. Alone with her animals.

* * *

Mollie was on pins and needles all day, heading up to the charity event. Beck stood in the kitchen waiting for her when she emerged from her room. She felt very self-conscious and wasn't sure how he would react when he saw the dress. It was so beautiful; she loved it, even though she felt a little spoiled liking it. It was just uncomfortable; she wasn't used to it but it made her smile. As she walked out into the kitchen, he had lifted a glass of water to his mouth and he let it drop. He set the glass back on the counter. His expression was one of extreme appreciation and she felt a feminine jolt of triumph that she had never felt before rocket through her. *He liked her dress too.*

"Mollie, you look beautiful."

She smiled. This was the most wonderful moment, seeing the sparkle in his eyes. "Thank you. I really like it. I wasn't sure if you would or not."

He walked toward her. "Wow! What's not to like? That color makes your beautiful eyes even more vibrant and your pretty hair just sparkles. And the dress fits you like it was made for you. You're gorgeous. But you are always. The dress just fits you…tonight, it just makes you a vision."

She tried to not let herself get too unsteady by his wonderful words. She had given herself a good talking-to. And though she was going to let herself have a wonderful time tonight and though she was not going to let herself worry too much, she still didn't need to fall too far down into the rabbit hole. That would mean climbing back out would be terribly hard.

"I'm glad you like it. You look amazing too. But I knew you would. And like you said, I like you in your jeans and T-shirt and cowboy hat. And your boots."

He held up his leg. He had on a pair of black boots. They were fancy; she didn't know what they were made out of, but they were pretty. "I still have on my boots, just not my work boots."

"I like that. I decided not to wear my boots tonight." She lifted her skirt, showing her leg and the

221

pair of sparkly, extremely expensive shoes she had on. "I have Cinderella shoes on tonight. Because I kind of feel like Cinderella tonight."

"And I feel like your prince tonight. Shall we go? The family will be waiting at the airplane."

"Ready when you are."

He held out his arm and she locked arms with him. She slipped the beautiful purse that she had also bought over her shoulder, and they walked out the door. He helped her into his truck. It was hard for her to climb into it, so, to her surprise, he scooped her into his arms and set her in her seat.

"Easier that way. Plus, I get the benefit."

She smiled and he grinned. Then he closed the door and strode around the truck. They met the family at the airplane strip. All of the women looked beautiful. They all hugged her and everyone talked at once. She felt happy and they made her feel comfortable. Beck was flying them, but she thought he looked as if something were bothering him.

She stood beside Blaze, and Beck moved to stand beside the stairs.

"It's time to load up," he said, just as a limousine drove down the road toward them and pulled to a stop. Everyone watched as the driver got out. He was an older man.

Blaze leaned in. "That's my dad. I'll have to introduce you, but right now, you're about to get introduced to Granddaddy Talbert. If you're wondering why Beck looks so nervous, that's why. They haven't seen each other since all this started."

She looked at Blaze. "Thanks for telling me. I was wondering why he looked like that."

The older man who got out of the limousine was handsome for his age, which looked like late seventies or early eighties, she thought. He was just like she would picture a rich, older oil man, with his white hair and his Western cut suit and fancy boots. He strode across the parking lot to them, everyone welcoming him.

He walked straight up to Beck. "Hello, grandson. It's nice to see you again. It's been awhile. And this must be your Mollie." He looked at her and smiled.

Mollie hadn't known what to expect from a man

who had forced his grandchildren to marry. But she liked him immediately. There was a genuine spark of kindness and mischief in his eyes. Or maybe she was just a fool and couldn't tell someone's character at a glance.

"This is Mollie," Beck said, stiffly, but he gave her a small smile.

"I'm Beck's grandfather, Talbert McCoy, and it is a pleasure to meet you." He held out his hand and she placed hers in it. He covered her hand with his second hand and didn't let go.

"It's very nice to meet you, sir. Beck's told me a little bit about you, but it's really nice to meet you." She babbled, halting when she realized what she'd said.

He laughed. "Well, I'm sure you've heard several different things about me from him, so I'm glad you still like me anyway."

She heard other chuckles and was relieved she hadn't completely messed up. She wanted Beck and his grandfather to overcome their differences. "I do."

"A man in my position is used to people hearing

all kinds of things about him. But the one thing you need to know, young lady, is that I love my family beyond anything in this world. And I only want the best for them. I will go through whatever I need to in order to make sure that they are happy. And I have to say that you have brightened my day immensely. I'm glad to have you in the family. I will look forward to getting to know you a little bit better this evening."

"Yes, sir. I look forward to that too."

"Good." He released her hand.

"It's time to load up," Beck said, not looking happy. "I've got to get us there on time."

With that, he led the way up the stairs. He paused, turned, and held his hand out to her. "Let me help you up these stairs, Mollie. Wouldn't want you to trip in those shoes."

She reached for his hand—glad, she had to admit, that she had him to help her up and glad to not be the center of attention any longer.

Within minutes, everybody had taken seats. She sat near the window and Caroline took the seat beside her. Which was a relief. She had been afraid that

Granddaddy Talbert would have taken the seat beside her. She would have been a complete nervous wreck by the time the plane landed in Austin.

He did, however, sit in the seat across the aisle from her, and it was easy enough for him to turn and talk over his shoulder to her. Thankfully, with everybody else there, the conversation never completely focused on her until he asked her how everything was going at the farm.

She realized then that he was keeping up with what was going on at her ranch.

"Well, the peach trees are doing good. And my garden is, too. And we got my donkey, Sally, a few days ago. And she's just doing great, but I'm having a bit of trouble getting her to stay with the calves. She's only been here two days and she's supposed to stay with my calves at night, but she stays by the fence and waits for me to come pet her. But we'll get it all worked out. She's a real hoot."

Everybody laughed and Granddaddy Talbert did, too.

"I remember when me and J.D. were boys, we had

us a donkey. We loved that donkey and he followed us everywhere. He was a mean little hoot, too. But we loved him. We tried to ride him every once in a while, and he'd buck us off. It was the funniest thing and it really riled J.D. up. J.D. thought he could ride anything, but that donkey did not like to be ridden and they had an ongoing rivalry. I hope your Sally is a little tamer than that."

"Well, she doesn't like Beck that much. He said he thought at first, he had made a mistake getting her because she isn't real receptive so far to anybody but me. Not that there's anybody at the house to put her to the test except me and Beck. And she likes me a lot."

Caroline grinned. "Mollie, that's because you're just about the sweetest thing there is. And I think that Beck's right, because he told me that Rufus said you have a way with animals, so you probably do."

"I think they just know I adore them."

Granddaddy Talbert smiled at her and nodded. "They can tell."

The plane landed almost as soon as it had taken off and there were limos waiting for them. Beck sat beside her as they were whisked from the ranch's private airfield to the event. A huge tent was set up on the grounds near the lake. It was a beautiful place and there were lights everywhere. She had her arm in Beck's as the whole family walked in. People turned to welcome them.

Beck placed his hand over hers. "Relax. We're going to have a wonderful time."

She looked into his eyes and she knew that tonight was going to be her fairy tale.

CHAPTER SIXTEEN

They danced and she reveled in being back in Beck's arms. Dancing with Beck was her fairy tale. Exactly how she had hoped it would be. His family had made certain that she was made to feel welcome but even if they hadn't, Beck had been the perfect gentleman: constantly at her side, keeping her dancing, offering her something to drink, taking her out on the patio that had been built outside the large white tent so that instead of under the lights of the tent, they were under the light of the beautiful moon. She wondered how such a spectacular moon just happened to be shining on this particular night, as if someone had ordered it up just for them.

Beck held her hand and she fought down the

butterflies that had become constant inside her. And when he looked at her, she almost felt as if he actually cared about her—not just was friendly, but actually cared. She knew she cared; she knew she had fallen in love with Beck and there was no getting around it. She liked the sweetness of him; she liked the orneriness of him. And she felt for him and the dilemma he was in with his grandfather. She loved how he protected her.

Yes, she had to keep reminding herself that this was all fake, that they weren't going to remain married. But that didn't stop the truth, which was that she loved him. She would always love him, even after the fairy tale ended. Beck McCoy had a generous heart. He was just caught between a rock and a hard place in this situation with his grandfather. She was grateful for everything that his grandfather had done because it enabled her to be a part of this amazing man's life. And she just prayed that somehow, she was able to give back to him even a small portion of what he had given her. And she knew she could not let silence remain between them when it came to his grandfather.

To her surprise, Beck took her in his arms. His arms were looped lightly around her waist and clasped at the lower part of her back. She lifted her arms and wrapped them around his neck, because why miss the opportunity to hold Beck McCoy in her arms?

"Are you enjoying yourself?"

"I am. How about you?"

"More than I have before. You've been a hit—you know that, don't you? Everyone likes you."

She had gotten to speak with a lot of people and had been introduced to so many people she would never remember names. But it really didn't matter because she would never see these people again after this event. "That's nice. I tried to, you know, use my manners and not be all country."

He laughed, throwing his head back just slightly, then shook his head and looked back at her. "You know you are perfect in every way."

Her heart squeezed. Oh, she knew she wasn't perfect but that he would make such a statement thrilled her beyond measure. She bit her lip, wishing she could kiss him. Wished she was really his and that was something she could do on a whim. But she wasn't his and she couldn't kiss him on a whim. She had done that before and the only one who was going to be kissing on a whim would be Beck; she had already made that decision.

And as if he had heard her decision, he bent his head and kissed her lightly on the lips. Oh, she kissed him back, but she fought the need or the want to get all crazy with the kiss. That was just too dangerous. She was just grateful for this moment of feeling his lips on hers once more. She would set into memory all the kisses that he had given her and later, when she was lonesome, she would remember.

He broke the kiss off far too quickly. They were secluded slightly behind a palm by the edge of the patio, and yet there were people around. "You know, I could get used to that."

"Yes." His words put hope in her heart and it was so dangerous. She couldn't rely on that—on hoping for something that would probably never actually happen. "Beck, this thing between you and your grandfather that has you so determined to not make up with him...don't you think it would be good if you settled it? I mean, this thing between you and me hasn't been terrible. You've helped me and like you said from the beginning, you've been such a blessing to me, I could never repay you for what you're doing for me. I was just thinking that your granddaddy hasn't really done something completely terrible. Can't you make up with him? Can't you let it go?"

He tensed as she spoke, and she knew she probably shouldn't have said anything.

"Mollie, I will say what you and I have experienced hasn't been terrible—it's been great. Much, much more than I ever could have anticipated. I can't ever be mad about the fact that I met you. That you've been very good in my life. But there still remains the fact that my granddaddy forced me to do something that he had no right to force me to do."

Something in her clenched tight. "But Beck. He didn't actually force you. You had a choice. You could have chosen to walk away, to start on your own again...to leave it all behind. I know it sounds terrible and I wouldn't have gotten the blessing of meeting you or saving my ranch, but if this thing between you and your grandfather makes you so unhappy, then maybe you should have walked away. But your granddaddy's only going to be here for so many more years and then, like my granddaddy, he's going to be gone. That's just the truth of it. Life doesn't last forever and you have to make good choices. One day, you might regret things and realize that losing your relationship with your granddaddy wasn't worth it."

He dropped his arms from around her and she regretted so badly that she had opened her mouth. But then, that was selfish on her part. So very selfish. Still, she continued; she had started it, so she might as well end it. "Your granddaddy...he loves you. He took a risk making the decision to try to see you happy. I talked with the girls at the spa that day and I tried to understand exactly what was happening. They all told me that your Uncle J.D. and your granddaddy had everything money could buy, but they also had the loves of their lives.

"When it came down to it, they knew being loved by their wives was the most important of everything. That they'd been blessed. They had all the money—all the oil, all the businesses, all the things this world has to offer—but it was the love of their wives they cherished the most. He just wants you to be happy. Caroline told me she had been furious that Granddaddy had saved you and her for last because he had known that you two would be the most stubborn. You being the very most stubborn. I think you need to make up with him. So there, I said my piece—I could hardly help it. I care about you, Beck. I care about you so much and I'm..." She almost told him she loved him, but she couldn't.

He didn't want his grandfather to have his way. It was heartbreaking to her. She really let the truth settle in around her. She and Beck had no future because he would walk away in the end.

"I just wished that maybe you would open your heart enough to hear what I said. Before you have regrets."

* * *

Beck stood on the edge of the dance floor, feeling like dirt. He watched the dancers without seeing them. His thoughts were completely on Mollie. Everything she had said kept rolling through his head. She made a lot of very valid points, and yet he couldn't let it go. His granddaddy had overstepped his boundaries and he was not the guy who was going to just let that go like his sister and his brothers had done. And yet, letting Mollie go, he knew, was going to be the hardest thing he had ever done. But he would. He would do it because it was what he said he would do.

She had gone to the restroom and was probably hanging out somewhere with his sisters-in-law and his sister. Probably in no hurry to get back to him after their argument out on the patio. It was for the best; they were getting too close and he couldn't let himself get any closer to her. He needed to pull back in a major way.

"I like her."

At the sound of his granddaddy's voice, Beck stiffened and turned his head to see Talbert McCoy had stepped up beside him.

"I like her, too. There's nothing not to like. Mollie is salt of the earth. She's good. She's gracious, sweet, and she was in a bad way, so I helped her out."

"I'm glad you did. You have a good heart, Beck. You chose well."

"I didn't choose her for anything other than helping her." He gave his granddaddy a stern look, relaying to him that it hadn't been for love and he shouldn't get his hopes up. He didn't care whether he got his hopes up or not.

Granddaddy studied him—with sadness, he thought. That was odd. Of course, his brain immediately went back to everything that Mollie had said. That his granddaddy had acted out of love. That was some way to show it, was all Beck could think. "You have something to say, Granddaddy? Because I'm thinking this party is about over and it's time to head home."

"I agree. Beck, you always were the stubborn one. But I'm just going to say this and I know you're probably going to ignore me. I was afraid all along that you would probably be the one who wouldn't listen to your heart. That you would do it just to get back at me. That's why I had to be so ruthless when it came to your business, because I knew that was the only way you might even attempt to stop thinking about the business and start thinking about something other than just building a business."

Beck was ready to leave.

"To be honest, son, if this isn't right between you and Mollie, then that's fine. I just wanted you to see that there's more out there than work. I'm very pleased that you've helped Mollie in such a way. I've been keeping tabs on all that's going on about that and I think that she's going to be able to be fine after y'all split up. I was thinking that you might think about doing some grapes out there. Imagine running a vineyard might be a little bit more than she can handle, being on her own after you leave. But have you ever thought about that she could lease some land to the McCoy Stonewall Jelly Farm and Winery and have that income as a base and a buffer? She's got a little bit of land; to lease it could help sustain her in slow times. They'd give her a good price. I talked to Todd and them about it, and we could supplement if there's a need, but I doubt that there will be. I think it will come out to where it's a decent price for a good trade. Just a thought. Even if a long-term marriage and great-grandchildren don't come out of this union like I hoped, I just want to tell you that you chose well in helping her. She's a good person. I like that us McCoys are able to help people."

Beck realized Granddaddy had a great idea. His conversation with Mollie rolled through his head. "Well, I'm not happy about what you've made me do. Or what I chose to do after what you tried to make me do." What Mollie had said was true; he hadn't been *made* to do this—he had *chosen* to do it to help her. "I'm glad if the one thing that came of it was to help Mollie secure the land that had been in her family all of her life. Seems to me there's a lot of that going on in these parts nowadays—land that's been in families for generations is being split up. It's sad and I hate it, so for that I have to say this has been worth it." There, he at least admitted that.

Granddaddy's lips turned up in a solid smile. "It's good to know. Makes me think there's other folks out there I can help."

"Don't tell me you're thinking about...no, you're surely not going to go help somebody hold onto their land but meddle in other people's lives too?"

Why did he suddenly see his granddaddy out there, trying to force other people to get married?

Granddaddy smiled. "I didn't say I was going to do it, but I am thinking about some things. I'm going to retire soon and I'm getting tired of going into the office. I'm probably going to hand the reins of all this business over to you boys. Y'all can handle it however you want. That's going to leave me with a lot of time on my hands. I'm just looking at all my avenues, all my options."

Talbert gave him a very odd smile, one that told him that his brain was working as he winked and then walked away.

"If you see any of the others, tell them we're loading up in twenty minutes."

His granddaddy held a hand up and waved without turning back to him, acknowledging that he understood. He watched his granddaddy go and wondered what in the world he was up to.

CHAPTER SEVENTEEN

The next few weeks went by and Mollie had withdrawn. She had forced herself to do it. She knew that she was going to be broken-hearted enough when Beck left, and she knew without a doubt that he would be leaving. It hadn't been hard to withdraw because Beck had also withdrawn.

It was as if after her talk he had decided that they needed distance. Oh, they were still together; they were still working. They still got up in the morning and had coffee, but both of them were more distant, more reserved. And she assumed this was the latter half of their three months as they prepared to separate from each other. They worked hard and she knew he was making sure everything was ready for his departure from her life. She recognized it now. The goodness in him couldn't leave her unprepared; everything had to be perfect.

The peach orchard was finished. The irrigation was working well and in the near future, she would have a working peach orchard. She had all the equipment she needed to maintain it and, according to him, with everything else they were doing, she would have the funds to hire people to help her as needed.

Then he had turned his attention to the acreage that he suggested early on could be a vineyard. And he'd gone to work. He'd used the tractor, the new tractor that he had bought that was just big enough to handle the work it needed to do and that she could handle. It had all kinds of attachments, and she didn't even ask how much it cost. She could back up and connect the attachments without even getting her hands dirty. It was the fanciest thing she had ever seen, and he had taught her how to do everything. He was preparing her. It was in those times when he was teaching her how to run it that she had to fight the urges that came over her. The ones that had her wishing she could kiss him and put her arms around him and hold onto him forever, begging him not to go. She had sleepless nights; she always woke up the next morning determined that today she would be independent and not needy. She refused to be needy. She would stand on her own two feet; she would let him go. She would hold her head up high and make a success from the opportunity he had blessed her with. And in the end, what was an inconvenient marriage for him would be a blessing for her, just like they had originally planned.

They worked on the vineyard, plowing the fields, getting the plants and planting them. That was a chore; the two of them worked for days planting. And then Todd and Ginny had come over and gave them expert advice on everything they were doing. That's when Beck had told her that they had an offer to make her. And they'd offered her to lease the land and the plants, and they would send their people over to maintain them. They would pay her a very generous price to lease the land and harvest the grapes and she wouldn't have to worry about anything. She would have money coming in every month to help her have income. They had a second offer: they said it would take a while for the grapes to grow—it would be a few years—but they were willing to lease the land while the vines were young. She would get the money and they would tend to the grapes and teach her, and then they would have rights to a few years of the grapes when they started producing and then she could take over. That was an amazing offer. She wasn't even sure it was a viable offer from them.

Something told her there was something else going on with the offer. But she didn't say anything. This was the McCoys she was dealing with, and they had their own way of doing things. But she took the offer—the one Beck told her she should take, so she was secure in knowing that she now had an income coming in that would help her rest easy. It would also help him rest easy, she knew, and that was her main goal: for him to walk away, assured that she would be fine.

She ignored the voice of panic that kept begging her to tell him her true feelings, the voice that kept telling her to beg him to stay.

She was not listening to that voice. She was a strong, independent woman who had been through a lot and she refused to go down like that.

* * *

They had two weeks to go before this marriage was over. Beck had been flying more the last week. He had been working day and night to get everything set up for Mollie before he left. They were at a point where the setting up was all done. She would have income coming in from all kinds of projects. He just hoped she would be able to handle all of it. He had stressed to her that with the new contracts she had signed with Todd and Ginny that she would have the money she needed to hire help. She had almost gotten mad at him that evening, telling him he didn't need to be worried about her, that she was capable of taking care of herself. That she would be fine without him.

They stared at each other for a long moment after that conversation and he knew that he was going to have to let it go. She would be fine. He hadn't brought it up again and yet his gut twisted every time he thought about it. He cared for her; he knew that he cared for her, but who couldn't care for Mollie? She was amazing. But that was what it was: he just cared for her and he wanted to make sure she was going to be okay.

By the time he arrived home late Friday night, she had already gone to bed. He stared at her door, wishing she had been awake. Wishing tonight they'd been able to talk for a few minutes.

He woke the next morning and she wasn't in the house. He walked out on the porch, looking for her. When he didn't see her, he walked across the yard to the barn and around the corner of the goat pen. He found her sitting on the ground, holding the baby goat that she was so fond of. The one that had been so very tiny but had finally started growing a little. She looked up when he rounded the corner and for the briefest moment, he saw pain in her eyes. It was gone instantly and in its place, he saw a determined fire burning in her beautiful eyes.

He wanted her to be determined; he wanted her to succeed. He wanted to see fire and ice in her, to know that she was going to be okay. He didn't want to see that vulnerable person who he had first met at the dance hall. *The one who needed him...* His thoughts snagged on that. She didn't need to need him. He should get used to that. *Was that what was bothering him?*

"Good morning. I got in late last night. Flying people all the way to Washington State and then waiting for them and flying them back is an all-day trip."

"Yes, I'm sure it is. It's a good way to get away."

Something about her tone told him she remembered the conversation about the charity ball and he had told her that when he didn't want to go to one he scheduled flights so he wouldn't have to go. He'd been booking longer and longer flights lately. Mollie was on to him but she wasn't going to say anything, and he wasn't either.

"How's your baby doing?"

"She's growing up. She's going to go to a new

home next week."

Shock ricochet through him. "You sold her?"

"Yes." She nodded. "I have all these animals for that reason. I can't get attached to them. That's not the way a businesswoman works. And besides, I sold her to a good family. They've got kids who will adore her, and she'll be very loved. So, I'm just getting in the last of my loving from her and getting her ready. She'll have some days of sadness—I will, too. We'll both grieve for each other a little bit, but she'll forget about me when those sweet kids start playing with her. She has a great, big, beautiful pasture to run and play in and lots of grass. It will be great. So, yes, I sold her. I've got a new batch of babies coming and I just can't keep everybody."

His heart clenched. He knew her words were as much for him as they were about the goat. She was preparing. He had to do the same thing. "Yeah, I see what you're saying. It will be the best thing for her. You've got new babies coming along—she would probably be jealous."

"Maybe. But people get over things like that."

He looked out across the pastures, toward the cows and calves, where it was safer than looking at her. He spotted Sally meandering among the calves. "It won't be long and it will be time to load up your calves. You'll have your first infusion of cash into your bank account when you do that. There's a lot of calves out there."

"That will happen, what, next month?"

"You know if you need my help, all you have to do is call me."

"I won't need you. I've been preparing and I've already lined up for Rufus to help me transport them. He's going to come with his trailer and load them up. And then we'll just take them to auction. I've been to auction before. I know a good price when I see one." She looked away. Her goat tried to lick her face.

He felt a knot of heaviness inside him that he hadn't expected to feel. "I'm glad you're going to be a success, Mollie Mae McCoy." He added her last name, realizing that she had said after the divorce she was taking back her old name. She would be Mollie Mae McCoy for only two more weeks.

She'd soon go back to being Mollie Mae Darling. *Why did that make him sick in his stomach?* "I'm going to go out and check on the irrigation," he said. "Do you want to come?"

"No thanks. I'll let you do that. I'm going over to the other side of the property...you know, where that ravine is. I've been thinking about berry vines. There's a lot of them over there and they grow wild. I want to go and check them out. I'm thinking that that's something else I can do. This is going to be one heck of a farm you've got me started on, Beck McCoy. I can sell berries and peaches and strawberries. I want it to be that people come out here to pick their own if they want to. I've been thinking about all kinds of organic farming opportunities. I'm just a country girl who loves making jams with all sorts of different berries. Anyway, I'm going to go out and take a look."

"That sounds like a really great idea and you are a country girl...a darn good country girl—the best. Do you want me to come look with you?"

"No. I can do this on my own. You go check on what we've already done."

They held gazes for a long moment. *She was cutting him loose.* "Okay. I'll see you at lunch?"

"Yes, lunch. I'll see you at lunch."

She didn't show up for lunch. He decided not to go look for her because she clearly wanted some space and he had a meeting at his house.

Cal Emerson, the family lawyer, was meeting him there to hand over the divorce papers. Beck hadn't wanted to meet with him here at the ranch. It just didn't feel right.

Nothing about the divorce felt right. It just felt like something that had to be done.

So, with a glance about the place, he tamped down his desire to go talk to Mollie. He got in his truck and headed back to his ranch. His home. The only problem was, it didn't feel like his home anymore.

* * *

By the time Beck got home, feeling riled up and depressed after getting the divorce papers, it was six o'clock. The sun was on simmer as it headed toward a sunset that promised to be spectacular. He knew the moment he parked the truck that Mollie wasn't home. The ATV wasn't parked by the barn and her work boots weren't by the door where she left them rather than trail dirt into the kitchen.

This time, he didn't hesitate; he went looking for her. He called her phone several times, but she didn't answer. His mood was already sour, and this didn't settle well with him. He put his truck in drive and headed through the ranch toward the ravine. If she didn't want him around, that was fine, but she needed to at least let him know she was working late. He'd been thinking about her being out here alone, working by herself for a while now, and it was eating a hole in his gut.

He reached the area where the ravine cut through the ranch. It was deep and wide and full of overgrown scrub trees and underbrush and had steep drop-offs that cut down to the creek that ran through the middle of it. Right now, it was small but when the rivers flooded, it was even more dangerous to toy with. He drove along the overgrown road that got little use and wondered where she was. Feeling anxious, relief sprang up in him when he finally spotted the ATV among the tall grass.

He was out of the truck quickly when he didn't see her anywhere. He jogged to the ATV, yanked out his phone and called her again. He'd called Caroline on the drive across the ranch, but she hadn't heard from her. He hadn't wanted to worry anyone, but he'd needed to know if maybe she'd reached out to his sister.

When he heard her phone ringing from the ATV, he looked at the floorboard. His heart sank when he saw it. *All this time, she hadn't had her phone.*

Beck's mouth went dry. And as he picked the phone up, his fingers trembled.

"Mollie!" He started looking for her footprints. Within moments, he knew something was wrong.

His phone rang. "Beck, it's Jesse. Caroline said you were looking for Mollie. Have you found her?"

Beck was not a man who panicked but he was starting to. Jesse had been the sheriff of Stonewall for years before giving it up to take over a boys ranch and marry Caroline. "I haven't, Jesse. Her ATV is out here next to the ravine, and her phone was in it. I was just about to call you and the others. I need y'all out here. Can you round everyone up? Mollie is missing."

He hadn't called his granddaddy, but he'd called his brothers and sister and within the hour all his siblings and most of his cousins, who were in town and could come to help search for Mollie. That meant everything to him. Morgan and Amber were traveling, and Denton was on tour and Blaze was with him. But Jesse was here with all of his years as a sheriff behind him and was getting everyone organized for an extended search.

They'd all gathered around listening to Jesse when Beck spotted his granddaddy's truck barreling across the pasture. It wasn't his limousine; it was his truck. And when it pulled to a halt, his granddaddy climbed out of the driver's seat. He wore boots and jeans and a long-sleeve shirt and his cowboy hat, and he looked ready for battle.

"Why did nobody call me about this? I went into the diner to get some pie and Dixie was about to have a fit, she was so worried. She told me that she had heard through the grapevine that Mollie was missing and that you had all gathered out here to look for her."

Beck nodded. "Yes, sir. I came home and I can't find her. Her ATV was out here where she'd been working. Her phone was in the ATV but she's nowhere to be seen. I've been looking for her for over two hours."

"Well, I might be old but I'm not too old to help search for my granddaughter-in-law. So y'all get this show on the road and tell me what you need me to do. And where the heck is the sheriff's department?"

Jesse stepped in. "Come on, Talbert, relax. She's only been missing for a few hours. There's a wreck out on the interstate, so they'll be here when they can. I'm here and we've got a lot of good help to get started. We'll have a bigger search party later but right now I don't want people trampling everything to death. There's a lot of underbrush and I want us to do this in an organized manner. We don't have a lot of daylight left, so everybody gather round.

"We're going to go in teams of two. This ravine is

dense, so half of us are going to go down one side of the ravine and the other half's going to go the other way. And Talbert, I know you want to go down there, too, but you're not going to. You're going to wait here in case she shows up. Or if we need you to bring the ATV alongside the ravine in case we need it to get her out quicker. Do you understand? I don't want any guff from you."

Beck saw the aggravation in his granddaddy's eye for the fact that he wasn't going to be involved in the actual search and rescue down in the ravine. But Beck knew what they were asking him to do was hugely important. The last thing they needed was his granddaddy hurting himself in the ravine; it was steep and there were places that a person could fall easily. He feared that something like that might have happened to Mollie, and she was lying somewhere, knocked out and needing him.

"Granddaddy, it's where you're needed." He said the words quietly but with force.

His granddaddy calmed. He was used to taking charge, used to doing things his way, but he wasn't going to get his way this time. "Okay. I'll stay here, but you better all have your phones on and be ready. And if you see something, you let me know."

Beck nodded. "We will. You get all your emergency numbers ready. You know how to drive that thing?"

"I never met anything I couldn't drive, son."

"Okay then, come on y'all, let's get this started. I don't want Mollie down there at dark." His gut told him that something terrible had happened. He was the odd man out. Morgan and Amber weren't there, and Holly was with the kids. Allie had dropped hers off with Holly, and she was with Wade. But Ash had no partner, so Beck went with Ash. He was glad because Ash was a vet and that was almost as good as a doctor, right?

They all spread out; everybody entered the canyon a certain distance apart and they started their walk. Ash and Beck started at the farthest end from everybody, where he had last left off his search. Everybody else would be coming behind him in case he and Ash missed something along the way.

He and Ash made their way down the steep ridge. It was getting rougher and steeper the farther they went, and he knew that the creek bed was widening. The ravine would eventually lead into a wider creek area that would lead into the river, but that was a long distance from this ravine. Mollie's property was unlike the McCoy property that sat closer to the river; she was a good distance away. He was startled when he looked up and saw Sally slowly picking her way down the slope up ahead of them.

"Where is she? Look, even her donkey is worried about Mollie." He stared at Ash, feeling as if his world was crashing in around him.

"Hang in there, brother." Ash's said. "She needs you to hang in there."

"Ash, I can't..." Emotion clogged his throat and he knew he couldn't lose Mollie. He had been kidding himself for the last month and a half, ever since the dance...since they had started distancing from each other, each preparing themselves for this departure. He had been telling himself that he could walk away—that he *would* walk away. But now her words rang in his head. Words she had spoken often that one day his grandfather would be gone and he would regret losing him. He understood her words now, only this wasn't about Granddaddy, this was about losing Mollie. *Had he lost Mollie?*

He needed Mollie. "Ash, I can't lose her. We have to find her." And with that, he started walking and yelling and calling her name.

* * *

It was dark when Mollie tried to sit up. She hurt all over and her skin stung. She blinked in the darkness, wondering where she was.

She tried to sit up again and a groan ripped from her. She realized she was lying in a hole. Fear raced through her. *What had she done?* Slowly, her thoughts got straight, and she remembered she had been looking for truffles.

She'd needed a distraction. She'd been working on the wild berries and she remembered her granddaddy saying that the ravine held secret treasures. Secret treasures that people paid a lot of money for. If someone wanted to spend the time to go down into the ravine and dig them up. She remembered he'd shown her how to find truffles. Restaurants paid great money for them.

And she'd decided to look for some.

It had been a long time ago and so she had started down. What she hadn't been expecting was how steep it was. She realized she might have been in the wrong spot because Granddaddy would have never taken her down this steep spot; he would have taken her down a safer route. When her foot slipped and then caught on a vine and she went down hard, she rolled through wild berry vines and rocks, and then she fell through the air. It was the last thing she remembered until now.

Now, everything was dark. She was in a hole. She called out for help and her words echoed. *Had she fallen into a cavern?* These hills were riddled with caverns. She called again. And fought being scared. The terror gripped at her, though. She did not like dark places. She did not want to think about what could be down here with her. And she hadn't told anybody where she was going. She moved her hand to her pocket and realized her phone wasn't there. She probably lost it on the roll down the hillside. She was in terrible, terrible trouble.

She closed her eyes. She knew Beck would come for her. He would come home and find that she wasn't there; he would realize that the ATV wasn't there, and then he would come looking for her.

She listened for any sounds that might terrify her further, like rattles of a rattlesnake. Thank God she didn't hear anything. She started praying—she prayed that she was the only thing down in the hole, and she prayed that Beck would find her soon.

* * *

The sheriff's department had come, and his granddaddy had called in more people. But Beck hadn't come out of the ravine. He knew that people were coming but it was getting dark out there in the trees; it was getting dangerous. He started to get hoarse. Ash was, too. His family was giving it their all and they were all keeping in contact. He had told them all to be safe, to not endanger themselves, but they were all still there—even his sisters-in-law and his sister. The McCoys were not giving up on one of their own. That's what Caroline had told him. Beck had about lost it when she said that. Sadly, he had almost given up on Mollie. He had been willing to divorce her just to make a point to his granddaddy. He was a fool. He was a blame fool.

He yelled her name again, "Mollie!" The words came out as a growl. And then he forced them out as a yell. His voice cracked with the wariness of it. They hadn't gone more than a half a mile but walking up and down was taking forever. The foliage was rough, and he and Ash were both scratched. He worried for his sisters-in-law and Caroline. Worry filled his brain.

"Did you hear that?" Ash asked and Beck looked at him. They both stopped.

"What?"

"Call her name," Ash said.

He hadn't heard anything; his brain had been too occupied with worry. This time, he yelled her name as hard and loud as he could and then he waited.

"Beck."

The word—he heard it. It was as if from a long distance, and yet it didn't sound as though it were that far away.

Beck and Ash started moving downhill, looking down. Sally charged down the hill past them.

"I hear her. She sounds like she's close, but far. Ash, I think she's underground somewhere."

"Caves." Ash stared at him.

"Yes!" Beck halted. *Caves.* Hill Country was riddled with caves. Caves were sometimes just holes in the ground. He heard it again; he heard his name. He started yelling then. He had the flashlight of his phone on, and he and Ash both started quickly shining their lights on the ground.

"Ash, call them and get us some stronger lights—weren't they bringing them?"

"Yeah, we'll get everybody here and the lights."

Suddenly up ahead Sally started hee-hawing loudly.

Beck charged forward and saw the little donkey

staring into a hole. Beck fell to the ground and looked into the dark hole that Sally had found. "Mollie, are you there?"

And then he heard the sweetest words he had ever heard.

"Beck, I'm here."

* * *

Mollie stared up into the darkness and then saw a very small light. It wasn't that far up, maybe five feet. Thankfully, it wasn't farther than that; she probably wouldn't be able to move right now. And thankfully she hadn't hit solid rock but dirt. In the light, she couldn't see Beck but she heard his voice, felt his presence, and she knew she was going to be okay. He called for her to be still, for her to hang on; he was coming down. And within moments, she heard other excited voices, people yelling her name. She heard Caroline calling for her to be calm and hang on; she heard Allie and Ginny and all the other voices that she had come to hold so dear. But most of all, she heard

Beck.

With a rope under his arms, he lowered himself into the cavern and then dropped the short distance. He had already asked her if she was okay, if she was hurt, and she had told him she was scratched up and very tender, but she didn't think she had anything broke. One look at him and she just grabbed him—slung her arms around his waist and held on. Despite every molecule of her body screaming at her not to cry, she did. She had thought in those moments after she woke and realized she was lost in a hole, that maybe he wouldn't find her. But he had.

"Mollie, I thought I lost you. Come on, let's get you out of this hole. Let's get you cleaned up. Let's take you home."

She nodded, unable to say anything. Ash dropped down into the hole as Beck wrapped the rope under Mollie's arms and they lifted her up so Jesse, Todd, and Wade could reach down. and pull her up out of the hole. Immediately, she was swarmed by all the people she loved, even Sally was there. Her heart swelled. Three months ago, she had no one. Her granddaddy had died and she had nobody. And now, at least for this moment, she had this wonderful family. While they were all telling her how glad they were that she was alive, the guys pulled Beck out of the hole.

Immediately, he scooped her into his arms. "Okay, everybody, let's get her up to the ATV and get her to the ambulance."

She laid her head against his shoulder, too exhausted to speak and overwhelmed. After they had made it up the ravine, she saw Talbert McCoy waiting in her ATV. They were probably over a half a mile away from her berry vines and he had driven the ATV and was waiting for them. There were other trucks there, too.

Talbert drove over the ATV; he reached out, patted her leg and gently squeezed it. "Darling, I'm glad you're safe. Now let's get you to an ambulance."

Beck had climbed in with her and held her in his arms. Everybody said they would meet them at the hospital. Granddaddy put the vehicle in gear and shot across the pasture with them. He didn't waste any time getting them back to the house, where an ambulance waited.

Within moments, she was loaded up and Beck climbed in with her. They were closing the door with Talbert watching them, telling her that he'd be at the hospital right behind them. Beck thanked his granddaddy and told him he would see him there. Her heart leapt in her chest as she saw that there didn't seem to be any animosity between them. Beck acted almost like nothing had ever happened between him and his granddaddy, and she had hoped that they had let all that go. Then again, she had a lot of time to think, sitting there on that hard ground. Just a little over two days—counting the night—and there would be nothing more to be mad at his granddaddy about: he would be divorced and have his life ahead of him.

He squeezed her hand. The EMT was checking her out and put an oxygen mask over her face so she couldn't talk. She was too weary to talk, anyway. But later they would talk. She laid back, rested her head against the cushion, and closed her eyes.

* * *

The doctor had admitted her for observation. She had

hit her head on her fall down and had a lot of scrapes and bruises and a few cuts from her fall. She ached all over, and so she didn't mind when they had given her some painkillers and restricted a lot of people in her room. Beck had been by her side the whole time, holding her hand and looking terribly concerned. She wasn't sure how to feel at the moment. The doctor had actually said she could be suffering from a little shock, too. Beck had been terribly concerned about that. The doctor had told him they needed to keep her calm, and he had nodded and then agreed. But he held her hand and promised her that when this was over, they would talk.

The medicine they gave her made her sleepy and she went to sleep with Beck holding her hand, telling her to relax and that everything was going to be just fine—everything was going to be great. She wasn't sure what they had put in her IV, but as she drifted off to sleep, she actually felt pretty great. But she knew that was only because the painkiller had kicked in; she knew when she woke up tomorrow that it would be one day closer to her divorce and there was nothing the doctors could do to help her through that pain.

Thankfully, when she woke the next day, Beck was still by her side, sleeping in a chair. She lay there in her hospital bed, enjoying looking at him. She wouldn't get to do this after tomorrow. When the nurse came in to take her blood pressure and her temperature, it woke him up; he jumped to his feet, startled. She couldn't help but chuckle. He looked so tired; he had probably just passed out, unable to stay awake any longer. She knew Beck would be one to worry and look out for her even though she was soon not to be his problem.

"Good morning, sunshine." She smiled at him. She did feel better this morning. Oh, she was sore but her head was clear, and she was grateful that nothing had been broken—grateful that he and all his family had found her.

He sank down into the chair after the nurse moved out of the way and took her hand. "Good morning."

His voice always sent a thrill through her; looking at him did, too.

"I guess they'll probably let me out of this joint

today. I feel much better. Thanks to you and your family finding me."

"Mollie, I wasn't supposed to upset you yesterday. But, Mollie, you can't go around, not taking your phone with you. And going down in that ravine by yourself…you should have never done that. Somebody needs to know where you're at. I was so worried—no, I was terrified that something horrible had happened to you and it had. You are so very lucky."

He was lecturing her as if he cared for her, and it made her sad. "Beck, I am about to live by myself. I'm not going to call somebody every time I want to go do something on my ranch—that's just not how it works. I just made a mistake and forgot my phone. I thought it was in my back pocket."

"I know you're used to being alone, but you can't do that. You need to let me know."

Her brows knitted and as the nurse exited the room, she tugged her hand from his. "Beck, I'm very grateful that you came and found me, but as of tomorrow, you're not going to be my husband anymore. I'm not going to be calling you every time I need to do something."

He took her hand again. "Mollie, listen to me. Mollie, I love you. I realized yesterday when I couldn't find you and I thought I'd lost you. I was horrified. And I thought about everything you said to me, about how if something happened to Granddaddy, and I hadn't made up with him, how much I would regret that. But it wasn't Granddaddy I was thinking about— it was you. That conversation we had together that you kept harping on it all came back to me. Mollie, I love you. I can't think about a world where you're not with me."

She couldn't move. He had just told her the words she longed for, she dreamed of. The words she thought were everything in the world that she wanted. But she clamped down hard on the desire to tell him that she loved him too. He was just doing this out of a need to take care of her. Out of worry and thinking that she couldn't make it on her own. Well, she could.

She looked at him. "Beck, I know this is emotional and I know that I scared you. And I'm really sorry. I know that you care for me. But you probably don't love me. I mean, if it took the accident to make you think you love me, knowing you, you're probably just confused and you're thinking you want to take care of me because you feel obligated."

It was true. She knew Beck; she knew how his mind worked, and this was all probably the truth. How could she ever know if he did love her or just felt an obligation? She couldn't.

"Mollie, I do love you. I knew I cared for you, but I've never loved anybody like that—I never felt that emotion. And you were right—I was so angry with Granddaddy, and I almost lost you because I wouldn't tell you I loved you because I was being spiteful to my granddaddy. Wow, I can't hardly believe that. And yesterday, I got a second chance. I knew that I would have made the biggest mistake of my life if I had let you walk out that door and out of my life. I had gotten home yesterday with the divorce papers in my hand but I ripped those things to shreds last night. I don't want our marriage to end."

She shook her head; she could not believe him. "Beck, you don't know how badly I wanted to hear those words. How I thought I would do anything to hear those words from you. That you loved me. But I can't let you do that. I would never know if you ever truly loved me. I would always wonder in my heart if you had just done it out of thinking I couldn't make it on my own. And guess what—I *can* make it on my own.

"Anybody could have an accident, which is what I classify yesterday as. I'm a very responsible person and I just had an accident. But I can't live my life in fear and I'm not going to be calling people all the time, letting them know where I am. If I want to go somewhere on my property, I will go do it. And, Beck, you don't have to feel responsible for me anymore. You've done what you said you would—you've set me up and given me this wonderful farm to live on and to make a living at, and even more possibilities and dreams. I don't want you because you feel guilty. I don't need you."

That was hard to say. Because the truth was, she needed him desperately. But she didn't want him out of guilt.

He stood, holding her hand and not letting go. "Mollie, I'm telling you, I've never meant anything more sincerely in my life. You are my wife and you are who I want. It's not out of guilt. It's not out of thinking you can't make it on your own, because I know you can. I believed in you from the beginning. I love you." He squeezed her hand and bent to kiss her fingertips. "And you love me. All you have to do is tell me and share this life with me that we almost let go."

She wanted to throw her arms around him so bad; she wanted to hold onto him and never ever let him go. She felt tears welling inside her. And then he sat on the side of the bed very gently; he eased to where he was looking straight at her. She couldn't speak; she could barely breathe. She wanted to run but she was in a hospital bed; there was no running involved right now. He reached his thumbs up and gently swiped her cheeks, and she realized that those dratted tears were falling from her eyes.

"Beck, I don't want you to ever regret marrying me. I need you to divorce me."

Gently, he cupped her face between his large

palms. His eyes held hers as he leaned forward and kissed her lips. It was gentle and sweet and wrapped around her aching heart. She did not let herself respond.

He pulled back and broke the kiss. "Please tell me you love me."

She shook her head. She wasn't going to tell him. He needed to walk away from her; she needed to let him go.

He smiled. "Mollie, you can't lie to me. I know you love me. Yes, I'm arrogant by saying that, but you do and you know you do. And if I have to get on my knees and grovel, I will." In that moment, he slid to his knees. He held her hand. "Mollie Mae McCoy, I promise that if you want me to divorce you tomorrow, I will sign those papers. And I will let you go if I have to. But I'm asking you right now, on bended knee and with all of my heart laid out here before you...I love you and I'm asking you to be my bride. Will you marry me? Will you let me love you for the rest of your life? Will you let me share your life? I can't wait to see what you do with your farm. And I mean that with all of my heart."

Her heart squeezed tight and she so wanted to be strong. But looking at him, his beautiful eyes gazing into hers, she believed him.

"Tell me you love me."

"I love you, Beck McCoy. I've loved you from almost the moment I met you. I just don't want you to ever regret—" She didn't get any more words out; he had come up off the floor and he was kissing her long and hard and with feeling. She wrapped her arms around his neck like always and kissed him back.

Moments later, he pulled back and rested his forehead against hers. "I am so thankful for you."

Mollie felt those stinking tears well up in her eyes again. *Had anybody ever told her they were thankful for her? Boy, she loved this man.* "And I am thankful for you. And very blessed."

The door opened and the doctor walked in. They looked at him; he was smiling. "Well, it looks like you two are about to get to head out of this hospital. You look good—I mean, you've got some scratches on you but you're fine. All your vitals are good and so we're going to release you. And there is a whole waiting room full of folks who cannot wait for you to get out of here so they can cheer you home."

Beck grinned at her. "Believe me, me not letting you go is going to make a lot of people happy out there."

She smiled with all of her heart. "They can't be happier than me. I was not sure I was going to be able to make it, letting all of y'all go."

"Come on, Doc, let's release her. We've got some celebrating to do."

"Yes, you do. While you two get back to doing what you were doing, I'll go get the papers ready. I'll let those nice folks in the waiting room know they'll get a chance to see her in just a few minutes."

As soon as he walked out the door, Beck sat back down on the side of the bed, took her hand, and kissed her ring on her ring finger. Then he looked at her. "We're going to get you another band to go with this ring. This time, it's going to be a forever band. And I was thinking that we might have an actual wedding— you know, where all the family can come, and we'll say our vows together in front of everybody. This time, it will be not because we're having to but because we're wanting to desperately."

She grinned. "I think that's a brilliant idea."

And then he leaned forward and he kissed her again.

About the Author

Hope Moore is the pen name of an award-winning author who lives deep in the heart of Texas surrounded by Christian cowboys who give her inspiration for all of her inspirational sweet romances. She loves writing clean & wholesome, swoon worthy romances for all of her fans to enjoy and share with everyone. Her heartwarming, feel good romances are full of humor and heart, and gorgeous cowboys and heroes to love. And the spunky women they fall in love with and live happily-ever-after.

When she isn't writing, she's trying very hard not to cook, since she could live on peanut butter sandwiches, shredded wheat, coffee...and cheesecake why should she cook? She loves writing though and creating new stories is her passion. Though she does love shoes, she's admitted she has an addiction and tries really hard to stay out of shoe stores. She, however, is not addicted to social media and chooses to write instead of surf FB - but she LOVES her readers so she's working on a free novella just for you and if you sign up for her newsletter she will send it to you as soon as its ready! You'll also receive snippets of her adventures, along with special deals, sneak peaks of soon-to-be released books and of course any sales she might be having.

She promises she will not spam you, she hates to be spammed also, so she wouldn't dare do that to people she's crazy about (that means YOU). You can unsubscribe at any time.

Sign up for my newsletter:
www.subscribepage.com/hopemooresignup

I can't wait to hear from you.

Hope Moore~
Always hoping for more love, laughter and reading for you every day of your life!

CPSIA information can be obtained
at www.ICGtesting.com
Printed in the USA
LVHW081806010720
659470LV00018B/926